"You were my lifeline to sanity."

Benedict got to his feet. "You and my writing. So don't go thinking that the money for Windfair came from or through my wife."

He had known Serena would think that, and hate the money for that reason. But at this moment she wasn't sure if Benedict's own money wasn't just as objectionable. "Leave me alone, Benedict," she whispered, covering her face. "Please."

Her hands came down as he moved to the door. "Benedict?" she said tightly.

"Yes?"

"How did Caroline die?"

Even across the room she could see the bleak shadow descend over his eyes. "She killed herself," he said starkly, and was gone.

Books by Elizabeth Graham

HARLEQUIN ROMANCE

HARLEQUIN PRESENTS

These books may be available at your local bookseller.

Don't miss any of our special offers. Write to us at the following address for information on our newest releases.

Harlequin Reader Service
P.O. Box 52040, Phoenix, AZ 85072-2040
Canadian address: P.O. Box 2800, Postal Station A,
5170 Yonge St., Willowdale, Ont. M2N 6J3

Passion's Vine

Elizabeth Graham

Harlequin Books

TORONTO • NEW YORK • LONDON
AMSTERDAM • PARIS • SYDNEY • HAMBURG
STOCKHOLM • ATHENS • TOKYO • MILAN

Original hardcover edition published in 1985
by Mills & Boon Limited

ISBN 0-373-02708-7

Harlequin Romance first edition August 1985

This book is lovingly dedicated
to the memory of
Pamela Galsworthy Whiteside
Her untimely passing diminishes
all who knew and loved her.

CHAPTER ONE

SERENA Howard stepped back from the easel and flexed her shoulder muscles as she surveyed the painting she had been working on, head poised critically to one side. The finishing details always created tension at the nape of her neck, and she rubbed it now with absently massaging fingers. The picture would do; its depiction of a Bermuda lane, twisting and bordered by high white stone walls draped in magenta bougainvillaea, would be snapped up by some tourist to the islands sentimentally inclined to re-live a brief sojourn in Bermuda.

She sighed as she cleaned off her fine detail brush and upended it into the drying jar on her glass-topped palette table, then sat down in the old but comfortable leather armchair that had been her father's, her eyes fixed on the painting she had just completed. In her art student days in London, she had never contemplated turning out her work with a view to its commercial aspect. But then, many facets of her life now had never been dreamt of in her passionately dedicated days at the Slade School of Art.

She hadn't known then that her big, bluff, fun-loving father would die in an unnecessary water accident and leave her desolate without his presence and stunned by the knowledge that foolish investments on his part had abolished with one sweep the gracious, indulged life she had always known in Bermuda.

Windfair, the sprawling mansion set in ten lawned and wooded acres of Paget Parish, had suddenly become a deadweight anchor hanging from her young neck. There was no way she could maintain the enormous house filled with her family's history, which stretched back to Peregrine Howard, who in the opening years of the eighteenth century had been licensed as a privateer by the English Government and had begun the building of Windfair with his profits. Serena knew, with a defeated sense of bitterness, that she would have to sell the property, probably to a business concern with an eye to its commercial value as an exclusive guesthouse, which had been the fate of many old Bermuda mansions.

Then late one sleepless night, the idea had come to Serena that she could do the same thing, given some backing, and retain her family home as well as provide an income for herself. Her background had fitted her for nothing but 'dabbling in paint', as her father had indulgently termed her passion, with no means of supporting herself, let alone the bulky Windfair estate.

So had been born Bermuda's most exclusive guesthouse, which was rapidly becoming renowned for its tasteful yet relaxed atmosphere in an historical setting. That Serena was herself a descendant of the notorious Captain Howard had been a drawing card of no mean proportions. Now that the everyday running of the guesthouse was performed smoothly by the competent staff she had found and trained, several hours of her day could be spent safely secluded down here in her studio cottage, an old pink-walled building which she had converted, when money permitted, into a functional apartment where she could be completely self-supporting, and often was when the main house was filled to capacity.

'Miss Serena?' a woman's deep voice sounded simultaneously with a sharp rap on the outer door. 'Are you in there?'

Serena smiled wryly as she got up from the chair and went to the door. 'Yes, Matty, I'm here—where else?' Opening it, she grimaced at the regal figure of Windfair's housekeeper, whose plump, dusky face was wreathed in a disapproving frown. Balanced on one arm was a tray of covered dishes, from which materialised the tantalising odour of crisply fried bacon and scrambled eggs, reminding Serena that she hadn't eaten yet this morning.

'Why can't you behave like civilised people?' Matty grumbled as she pushed past Serena and dumped the tray so hard on the small round table next to the kitchenette that the cup rattled noisily on its saucer. 'You can't expect to run a business on an empty stomach.'

'My stomach is perfectly happy with its diet of home-grown bananas for breakfast once in a while,' Serena retorted without rancour, 'and you know as well as I do that the place almost runs itself now.'

'That's not what the Johnson girl was saying from behind her fancy desk in the hall a few minutes ago,' the housekeeper said as she straightened, putting her hands on her ample hips to glare at Serena, venting her jealousy of the young and trim Pat Johnson who took care of everything from confirming bookings to arranging horseback rides along the trails leading from Windfair. Matty supposed, wrongly, that the younger woman had stepped into her place of importance in the household she herself had dominated for so many years. Not to be sidetracked from her present mission, she added caustically, 'And don't tell me you had bananas or anything else for breakfast, because I looked into your fridge yesterday and there was nothing but mouldy scraps of cheese and an inch of curdled milk in it!'

Unabashed, Serena wrinkled her nose. 'At least that way I won't get fat.'

'Huh! What you'll get is a thin little coffin in the ground!' Matty ambled over to look at the recently finished painting. Her pride in Serena's talent, which enabled her to paint scenes recognisable to herself, was unbounded. She was Bermudian born and bred, and fiercely chauvinistic; it surprised her not at all that visitors to the islands clamoured for Serena's work. Nowhere in the world was as beautiful as Bermuda, no other painter as skilled as the girl she had watched over as a replacement mother for the one who had died at Serena's birth. 'You've done this one again, that's good. It should bring a good price.'

A flash of irritation shot through Serena, surprising her with its suddenness. 'You make it sound as if I'm churning them out by the dozen solely for the cash they bring in,' she snapped, knowing that Matty would be hurt by the outburst, but unable to help herself. It was unfair too ... Matty had been her staunchest supporter when the money from her paintings had, indeed, been vital to the survival of Windfair at the beginning.

But the older woman took no offence. 'Eat your

breakfast, child,' she advised gently, going to the door. 'Don't worry about the tray, I'll send Cristy down to clean up later, now you've finished the picture.'

'Thanks, Matty.' The words of gratitude contained an apology as well, and Matty smiled, looking tired and every one of her sixty-eight years. 'By the way, what was Pat concerned about?'

Matty's expression came to avid life again at mention of her arch rival for supremacy at Windfair. 'She must have mixed up her book-keeping somehow,' she said slyly, 'because there's a man and his daughter arriving on Saturday and she's in a panic because she has nowhere to put them.'

'I thought bookings were easing off,' frowned Serena as she uncovered the largest of the plates and sat down before the meal that was beginning to cool.

'Not here,' Matty shrugged. 'Shall I tell her you'll be coming to see to it yourself?'

'You can tell her I'll be up soon to see if I can help,' Serena corrected firmly, knowing full well as the housekeeper took her bulk off with sudden energy that a peremptory order would be issued in her name, and that she would have to soothe Pat's ruffled feathers yet again. Matty was ridiculously, and unnecessarily, sensitive where the office manager was concerned. Pat was young, eager, and interested in her job, and Serena knew that she possessed a jewel among hotel staff. Sighing, she gave in to her hunger pangs and began her meal.

Later, having changed from the paint-spattered

loose top and well worn jeans she wore for
working into a straight linen skirt and matching
cotton-knit shirt in a beige colour that emphasised
the pale ash colour of her hair, she walked up
through the grounds of Windfair towards the
house.

As always, she took pleasure in the neatly
groomed lawns and the explosion of colour from
the purple and cerise bougainvillaea cascading over
walls and fences, hibiscus blossoms in orange and
red vying with the more delicate white of sweetly
scented frangipani. Brilliant beds of copper, gold
and butter yellow chrysanthemums were scattered
here and there on the lawns, and in the distance
the high fence surrounding the swimming pool was
rampant with the misty blue of morning glories.
An army of gardeners kept the estate in tip-top
condition, producing the vegetables used in the
dining room as well as the flowering beauty
abounding everywhere. Serena never ceased to be
thankful that she had managed to keep it intact,
and shuddered now as she entered the house by
the open terrace doors into the airy dining room.
By now, Windfair might have been carved up into
lucrative house and apartment lots, its uniqueness
gone for ever.

'Good morning, Pat,' she smiled to the girl who
leaned over the bookings register at the desk in the
vast central hall. Strikingly beautiful, the crisp
white of her sleeveless blouse complemented the
light brown of her skin, but her usual flashing
smile was absent when she looked up and returned
Serena's greeting reservedly.

Serena stifled a sigh of annoyance. Matty had
done her venomous work well. 'Having troubles?'

'If you can call having a full house trouble, then I've got it,' said Pat in the soft, lilting voice that nevertheless held a shade of resentment, which changed to dry question as she added, 'What did Matty tell you?'

'Just that you were having problems fitting everybody in,' Serena hedged, glancing down at the register. '*Are* we overbooked? If so, you can use my suite as usual, I can just as easily stay in the cottage.'

'I certainly haven't overbooked,' Pat said stiffly, 'whatever that old—woman told you. I'm simply trying to accommodate a man and his daughter from London without inconveniencing you. He telephoned this morning, and he'll be calling back in half an hour or so for his answer. He's never been to Windfair before, but he seems very anxious to stay here.'

'When are they arriving?'

'On Saturday. I think I can squeeze them into the Green Room overlooking the back, depending on the age of the daughter, of course.'

'No wife?'

'It seems not; at least, she's not travelling with them.' A thought struck the dark-eyed Pat. 'You don't suppose it's one of those kidnapping cases you read about, do you? Where an estranged husband steals his offspring from hated wife and disappears with him or her?'

Serena gave her assistant a despairing look. 'They're looking for people like you to write television plays, did you know? The most important qualification is an unlimited imagination, so you should do well at it.' She went on more seriously, 'No, I don't think he's an escaping, criminally inclined papa, but a tired businessman, possibly a widower, seeking a rest in the sun for two weeks.' Her brow creased as the looked down again at the register 'When your man calls back, find out the age of his daughter. If she's small, we can fit them both into the Green Room, it has twin beds. But if she's older, they'll have to take over my suite and have a cot in the living room.'

'Oh, that's good,' Pat breathed her relief, her smile breaking through the cloudy expression once more. 'Mr Ramsey sounds like a nice man—and not at all like the father of a grown-up daughter,' her eyes rolled expressively. 'Quite sexy, in fact.'

Serena's throat suddenly went dry as the name impinged on her consciousness. Her voice resembled a parched frog's when she croaked, 'What—name did you say?'

'Ramsey.' Pat's brows rose in surprise, but she glanced down at the pencilled note beside the telephone. 'A Mr P. Ramsey—do you think you might know him? He assured me he hadn't been here before.'

'No ... no, he hasn't been here.' Her vocal chords restored to normal, Serena concluded the conversation and made her way across the hall and back through the dining room to the kitchens, berating herself for her stupid assumption. There must be hundreds, thousands of Ramseys in the telephone books of Great Britain, so why had she leapt to the conclusion that it was Benedict Ramsey who would be arriving at Windfair this coming Saturday? Even if his first name had begun with the requisite 'B', Benedict possessed no daughter to accompany him on a recreational trip to Bermuda. At least ... She paused before

pushing open the swing doors into the kitchen.
There had been no daughter six years ago in
London. It was possible, of course, that he had
sired a child since then.

The kitchen staff worked at top speed in
preparation for the lunch that would be served an
hour or so from now, and the vast main
preparation room seemed hot and steamy despite
the cooling equipment she had had installed. The
huge wall ovens radiated warmth from the dishes
being cooked within, mingling with the spirals of
steam from large pans which awaited the
vegetables that would accompany them. Apart
from the resident guests who usually chose to
lunch and dine at Windfair, there would be a
sizeable influx of visitors to other hotels. The
enormous expense of renovation and expansion of
the kitchen area had demanded a greater return
from the dining room, and Serena had been
determined to have the best in local and
international cuisine to attract the kind of clientele
who would be willing to pay handsomely for the
privilege of dining at historic Windfair.

Tom Davis supplied the local touch with his
seafood and Bermudian recipes; short, very black,
and plumply rounded in the manner of most chefs,
he was fiercely protective of his special concoctions
and strongly resisted any efforts to pry his recipe
secrets from him.

Harold Welsh, on the other hand, was as
opposite in his appearance as in the dishes he
produced. Tall, thin, with brown hair escaping
from under his white lofted hat to flop damply on
his sallow brow, his special area was continental
cuisine, and he would confide his recipes to anyone

interested enough to ask ... somewhat tongue-in-cheek, because to Serena's knowledge no one had yet turned out the complicated dishes with quite his touch.

None of the other hotels would employ him either, Serena remembered drily as she watched the busy scene in the kitchen. Not because they disputed his skills, but because of his irreverent attitude to all who came within his orbit. Hotel manager or aristocratic guest, everyone received the same unabashed Cockney disregard for decorum. Now, seeing Serena, he dropped the cleaver with which he was finely chopping onions and celery for the pot bubbling on the stove to his left and sauntered across to her.

'Hello, darlin', checking on the galley slaves, are you?' Grinning at his own pun, he waved a generous hand at the bustling kitchen help. 'Everybody present and correct and doing what they ought to. Like to try my new sauce for the——?'

'No, thanks,' Serena hastily declined, moving forward to the wall table devoted exclusively to hot drinks. 'I just came for some coffee.' Shrugging, he went cheerfully back to his vegetables, and a moment later Serena left the kitchen bearing a small round tray which she carried upstairs to the sitting room of her private suite.

The bedroom of the two-room apartment had been hers all her life, and she had retained it when the renovations were under way, loving its familiar view of lawns and flowering trees at the back of the house. All through the year there was a constant parade of changing shape and colour, and it was quiet at the back. A sitting room had been salvaged from her one-time nursery next door, and she had always had her own bathroom.

She took her coffee now to the padded window seat, upholstered in the same bright yet soothing green and white cotton fabric which covered the casually arranged armchairs and sofa. The walls, too, were decorated in palest green, and added to the cool serenity of the room. Low bowls of fresh flowers adorned the coffee table fronting the deep-seated sofa, the polished walnut writing desk, the lacquered Chinese cabinet placed along one wall. Several of her early paintings, ambitious in their reach, were hung here and there around the room.

Ramsey . . . ridiculous after all these years to let that far from uncommon surname affect her. She had got over Benedict long ago, and hardly ever thought about those days in London. Days which had come to an abrupt halt when she had heard of her father's accident and come rushing back to Bermuda. Sipping the coffee she had poured, Serena reflected that it had been as well that she'd had the stupendous problem of Windfair to force her attention away from the bleak state of her emotions. There had been the ghastly realisation that Charles, her father, would no longer send his deep seafarer's voice booming through the hall as he went gustily out to wrestle the ocean; the rougher it was, the better it suited him.

Strangely, on the day of the accident there had been only a normal swell, enough wind to make his sleek yacht move easily, manageably. Shocked friends had told the equally stunned Serena that it had been a perfect day for sailing, especially for a man of Charles's skill. After discovering the

precarious state of Windfair's finances, the
thought had occurred to Serena that perhaps her
father had chosen not to return that day, but it
was too painful an idea to consider in detail.

And then there had been the trauma of
Benedict to cope with ... in its way, that was
almost worse. The dreams she had woven round
him, their future together. . . .

Her hand jumped convulsively when the telephone on a small side table flanking an armchair
rang shrilly, and the coffee she had scarcely
touched spilled into the saucer. Hastily setting it
down, she got up with a sense of relief and went to
answer. It wasn't often she indulged useless
memories, and Benedict was assuredly that.

'David?' Her brow cleared when she heard the
man's voice at the other end of the line, and she
cradled the telephone at her ear while she sat down
and tucked her slim legs under her, a smile curving
her lips. 'How lovely to hear from you.'

His voice, pleasantly husky, sounded an intimate
chuckle in her ear. 'If I'd known the welcome
would be so overwhelming, I would have come in
person.' There was a slight pause, then he went on
more soberly, 'Everything all right with you?'

'Yes.' That catch in her voice needed an
explanation, she knew, and she forced a wry little
laugh. 'Matty and Pat are at loggerheads again, I
don't know what to do with them. All I'm sure of
is that I need each of them in her own way, but
getting them to see it my way becomes more
impossible by the day.'

'It's not like you to—hang on a minute, Serena,
will you?' She heard an excited member of his staff
agitatedly tell him something, then his levelly calm

reassurance, and she smiled as she waited for the phone conversation to resume. To her, David's complete unflappability was one of his strongest points as owner of the Moongate Inn, a small but tremendously popular hotel in Hamilton. Its name derived from the stone circle garden decoration peculiar to Bermuda, its romantic appeal irresistible to the lovers of all ages who came to the islands.

'Serena? Sorry, about that. What were we saying?'

'It wasn't important. What was your original reason for calling me?'

'Oh. Well, just to ask if you're free for tennis this afternoon if I bring a couple over. They're very anxious to have a look round Windfair as well, and I said I'd contact you—even though they're certain to take their business to you next year.' He spoke with an assumed sound of being aggrieved, but both of them knew that by the time the couple next made their pilgrimage to Bermuda, it wouldn't matter which of the two places they booked into. David and Serena would have been married for months by then.

'As long as they're not tennis champs like the last ones we paired off with,' she groaned with genuine dismay. 'I've never been beaten quite so miserably, and we haven't played often lately.' Even if she had been willing to take time from her art, David always found it difficult to get away.

He chuckled. 'Don't worry, if they're champs at all it's of the retirement colony where they live in Florida. What?' He broke off again, and sounded exasperated when he said to Serena, 'Look, darling, I've got to rush, I'm sorry. Does four-thirty sound all right to you? I'd make it earlier, but these people are in their sixties, and I'm out of practice with lifesaving techniques if either of them has a heart attack from the heat.'

'Four-thirty is fine,' she smiled warmly, knowing that in any emergency concerning herself it would be David's calm assurance she would want. 'Oh— why don't you bring clothes for dinner, too? All of you.'

'You're sure? I think they'd love it, and I know I would.' His voice dropped a notch or two on the last words, and Serena felt the familiar warmth spread through her.

'Four-thirty it is, then,' she said unsteadily. ''Bye, David.'

Her hand rested on the receiver for a moment or two longer than necessary after replacing it on his, 'See you, darling.' She would have given anything she owned—except Windfair—to be able to address him in the same affectionate way. Yet she couldn't; it was as if she didn't trust herself to become that committed, despite their intention to marry the following June.

So few men would display David's restraint, she mused as she went back to her coffee and, grimacing at its coldness, decided to do without it. His patient ability to wait until her ardour matched his was part of why she loved him. And she did love him, she thought fiercely, although her responses to his lovemaking were slow in coming. That could be excused in a dozen ways ... shock at being deprived of her father and possibly Windfair at one fell blow, the agonising uphill climb of turning her family home into a viable commercial proposition. If it hadn't been

for David, Windfair as it was today might never
have existed, might indeed have been carved up
into precisely defined lots and buildings that
teemed with humanity.

It was David who persuaded his bank to
advance the monies necessary to convert Windfair
... David with his reputation for fair dealing in
his own business life. In a way, their situations had
been parallel ... his father had run the Moongate
Inn into the ground because of uninterest and
neglect, and after his fatal heart attack David had
forsaken his chosen career as a civil engineer in
England to rescue the dying hotel and build it into
the success it now was. David had the unique
ability to set aside his own personal problems and
concentrate on the needs of the moment. He had
made Serena's needs his needs six years ago,
doggedly bombarding the bank's officials until
they gave up—in frustration, Serena often teased
him.

But it wasn't for that that had brought her love
into being, nor for the unselfconsciously handsome
physique which attracted women in droves, as
moths to candlelight. Who could blame them? The
thick vigour of his reddish-brown hair underlined
his pure male appeal of broad competent
shoulders, chest muscles that gleamed like teak
when he emerged from sea or pool, waist and hips
tapered to meet long muscular thighs and legs
shaped leanly in the masculine style.

No, it was none of those, although each played
a part in the total man whose wife she would
become in a few short months. Perhaps the real
reason was that he was the antithesis of Benedict
in every way. He would never lie to her, as

Benedict had, never take the tender new emotions he himself had aroused and grind them into barren dust, as Benedict had . . .

Irritated that her line of thought had veered to that forbidden area, Serena jumped up from the chair and went to collect the tray of untouched coffee. She could find happiness with David only if she buried the past firm and deep in the oblivion it deserved.

'My, I hope I'm not the subject of your thoughts!' Pat gave a well acted shudder when Serena passed the desk on her way to the office marked 'Private' behind it. 'You look ready to kill!'

'What?' Serena shook her head to clear it. 'Oh. I was just thinking of something that happened years ago.'

'Or someone?' Pat questioned shrewdly. 'I'm glad it wasn't Mr Storey you were looking so murderous about. He's a nice man.'

'I wasn't contemplating murdering anyone,' Serena retorted, exasperated. 'You assume everyone has a past as lurid as your own, and you should watch that.' Her lips curved into a smile without her volition. Pat had been sought after by various men for several years now, but she was canny as well as beautiful. No man would ever make mincemeat of her emotions.

'I could write a book about it,' said Pat, rolling her warm brown eyes, 'but my mother would want to read it.'

'And I'm sure she could, idiot!' Serena laughed, her head turning then to the open hall doors when sounds of arrival floated through from the front parking lot. 'Now the stampede starts. I'll relieve you in an hour so you can have lunch.' She turned back to say casually, 'By the way, did you find out the Ramsey girl's age?'

Pat picked up one of the innumerable scraps of paper that lay around the telephone. It always amazed Serena that the other girl could find any information required from the slips at the touch of a finger. 'Yes, Mr Ramsey called back. She's eight, but he'd prefer that she have a separate bedroom.' She held up a hand to block Serena's frowning objection. 'Don't worry about it, I've solved the problem. There's an older couple coming on Saturday too, a Mr and Mrs Ellis. I had them assigned to the suite next to yours, but I'm sure they'll be just as happy in the Green Room, and the Ramseys can use the small room off the bedroom for the daughter.'

'Fine,' Serena said crisply.

Pat looked mournful, her eyes filled with compassion. 'Poor child, she'll want to be close to her daddy. Her mother died only last week, and I suppose he thought they both need a change of scenery.'

'Excuse me,' a middle-aged American man detached himself from the group that had entered the hall and came towards the desk. 'I made a reservation for lunch. The name's Walters, party of four.'

Pat's smile was immediate. 'Oh yes, Mr Walters. If you'd like to follow me, the dining room is just over here, or you can eat on the terrace if you prefer, it's just beyond the dining room . . .'

Serena sent an admiring glance after the trim-figured Pat; she'd found no need to check that the reservation had indeed been made. Smiling a little,

she went to the door marked 'Private' and entered
the small room that had once been her father's den
and which had now been turned into a pleasant
office. A battered old desk that had been used by
countless Howards over the years stood across one
corner of the room, giving Serena a view of both
door and French windows to her right. The small
garden just beyond the windows was meticulously
kept and exclusively hers, the only part of the
property apart from the cottage studio where
guests were not wanted.

For all the symmetrical neatness of the long
narrow lawn, a profusion of colour cascaded from
vines and shrubs and flowers at all seasons of the
year. Under a spreading poinciana tree, which
later would be smothered with reddish-orange
blossoms, stood elegant white wrought-iron garden
furniture. Only rarely did Serena allow anyone to
join her there; it was her private sanctuary where
she took the traditional afternoon tea completely
alone. High hedges surrounding the garden
ensured that no guest would wander into it
unaware, only the gardeners and herself possessing
keys to the solid wood door set into the side.

Serena had made the den look as little like an
office as possible, using antique furnishings to
hold the necessary papers and files instead of
clinical steel cabinets. Fresh flowers daily over-
flowed from desk, chests, tables; a framed picture
of her father, Charles, took a prominent place
beside the telephone on the desk. Two overstuffed
chintz armchairs flanked the small fireplace, which
also held an onyx vase filled with flowers.

Eyeing the stack of mail that had been placed on
the desk by Pat, Serena sighed faintly as she drew

it towards her. For some reason she was distracted today, and that irritated her. Far from the eager girl who had drunk avidly of life and love in London long ago, she was now generally cool and capable and in control of her life. She'd had to be that way; single-minded, purposeful, capable of making far-reaching decisions, or she would have fallen by the wayside and lost everything that was precious to her, everything that spelled security.

Pressing her mouth into a firm line, she slit open the first missive with an ivory letter opener yellowed with age. 'Dear Miss Howard,' the airmail letter read, 'I wonder if you remember our visit of two years ago? We so enjoyed staying in your lovely home, and I'm writing to ask if it would be possible for us to return . . .'

There were many similar letters, and Serena felt a swell of pride as she set them aside for Pat to answer. A slack period was rare at Windfair, even in the sometimes stormy winter months when many other establishments closed for lack of business. She liked to think that the ambience and warmth of the old mansion touched the lives of people as far away as the Far East, as close as England or America.

Unpaid accounts she added to the others in the drawer, making a mental note to write cheques the next morning. No one ever had to wait long for payment nowadays, as they had in the beginning when she had to distractedly juggle with one bill to pay a token sum off another.

A tap sounded at the door and Pat popped her short cropped head round it. 'All right if I go to lunch now? I have a heavy date at one.'

Serena nodded, smiling as she rose and came

from behind the desk. 'Who is it this time,' she
hazarded, 'the jazz man from Georgia or the
lawyer from London?'

'Neither. He's a schoolteacher from Oklahoma,
and I think he needs a good woman to bring out
his best points, which he hides under a stern
exterior. Why are some teachers like that,' Pat
prattled on as she led the way back to the
reception desk and picked up her waiting handbag,
'treating the whole world like a gigantic class-
room?'

'Perhaps that's the only way he can cope with
it,' suggested Serena, waving the other woman on
her way. 'Just don't forget that under that sober
exterior he's a man like any other. Don't be
tempted.'

Pat slanted her a pseudo-innocent look. 'In
broad daylight?'

'Just as many good women stumble in sun as do
in moonlight,' retorted Serena, her brow wrinkling
faintly in a frown as she watched Pat cross the hall
to the outer doors. What right had she to
moralise? At Pat's age of twenty-two, she herself
had loved a man in the deepest sense possible, and
had had two years to bitterly regret it.

CHAPTER TWO

NOTHING had thrilled the young Serena Howard more than to move into a cramped apartment to share with two of her fellow art students, Kerry and Joanna. Staying with friends of her father in a fashionable area of London hadn't been her idea of the independence she had dreamed of for years.

Charles, so bluffly unconcerned in other areas of his life, had been adamant that, if his only child must test her wings in the huge metropolis, she should do so under the careful eyes of the Wards, a childless couple of about his own age. They were kind enough in their own way, but their carefully ordered life for two was impossible to stretch and encompass a third member from a totally different generation. Conscious of the duty Charles had thrust upon them, they watched Serena as if she might explode at any moment, and made precise enquiries as to her whereabouts at all times of the day and night.

Serena had finally prevailed upon her father to allow her to move nearer to the art school. 'The two girls I'd be sharing with,' she wrote tongue in cheek, 'are from very good families and terribly dedicated to their art studies.' Both of these statements were true, but the last had an elastic quality that took in a wide-ranging social life as well as dedication to art.

Knowing that at last Life with a capital L was truly beginning for her, Serena made no objections

to being assigned the smallest of the three tiny
bedrooms. Avidly, she plunged into the whirl of
living as personified by Kerry and Joanna ... their
apartment was popular for late-night parties since
the landlady, who lived below, was deaf as a
doorpost and never noticed all the comings and
goings to the flat upstairs. The parties, in fact,
were rarely noisy affairs, since most of Kerry and
Joanna's friends were intellectual types who liked
nothing better than to sit far into the night sipping
wine and rearranging the world as they knew it.

Later, Serena would recall those evenings as being
boring in the extreme, everyone wanting to talk, no
one to listen. But in the beginning everything
enthralled her; the ultimate sophistication of her
flatmates, who made no attempt to disguise their
casual love affairs as anything but what they were.
Serena managed to hide her bewilderment at the
ever-changing parade of partners, but wasn't so
successful at concealing her own inexperience.

'My child,' Joanna, slim and tall and only two
years older than Serena, said three days after she
had moved in, 'I think it's time I explained the
dried flower arrangement to you.'

Serena stared at her blankly. 'The—what?'

'You've noticed the small bouquet that hangs
charmingly at one side of the flat door?' the other
girl questioned patiently as if to a backward child,
and when Serena nodded, went on, 'Well, when it's
turned to the wall, as it will be tonight, it means
that under no circumstances are you to enter the
premises.'

Serena's sea-green eyes widened still further. 'I
don't understand,' she shook her head slowly.
'Why shouldn't I come in? I live here.'

Joanna's thick mane of dark brown hair swung as she moved her head impatiently. 'I hadn't thought innocents like you still existed,' she marvelled, 'so I suppose I must explain the facts of life to you. Jeremy is coming here this evening, and we would—er—like to be alone. Understand?'

Her meaning penetrated suddenly, and Serena blushed a vivid scarlet, much to her own chagrin. What a naïve idiot she must appear to this girl who was only slightly older in years, but light years ahead of her in worldly experience. 'Yes, of course,' she covered up quickly, though not soon enough to avoid the half-pitying look that briefly crossed Joanna's dark eyes. 'I was thinking of something else, so I—how long am I supposed to stay away?' she tacked on breathlessly, again betraying her ignorance of how these things were done.

'Until the bouquet faces outward again,' Joanna explained gently.

Not knowing what else to do, Serena discovered parts of Chelsea she had never seen before, embarrassment dogging every step. How could she have been so gauche as not to realise that her flatmates would require privacy on occasion? The day might come, the night rather, when she herself would want to—entertain, for want of a better word. Her mouth twisted in a grimace of distaste, and she knew that she would never invite a man to the apartment with the express purpose of making love. There was something sordid, calculated, about what Joanna was doing tonight that was at odds with Serena's hazy ideas of how her love life would be conducted once it started.

Until now, there had been no opportunity to

indulge in more than a few kisses after a tennis club dance or a social occasion in one of the larger of Bermuda's luxury hotels. Her father, and the neurotically possessive Matty, Windfair's house-keeper, had seen to that. Her cherished freedom had been too dearly won for her to squander it in meaningless, and for her, somewhat grubby affairs. No, when the time came for her to surrender to the first real love experience of her life, it would be a grand passion to surpass all other passions, past and present. An experience that would reflect its fire in her work . . . she had accepted with resigned grace the criticism of one of her instructors that it lacked vibrancy and meaning.

Turning her steps homeward again, Serena went silently up the stairs to the apartment, and frowned when she saw that the flowers were still turned coyly towards the wall. Hesitating, she bit her lip and retraced her steps until she reached the street, where she paused and looked from left to right. What should she do now? A solitary man sauntering along on the other side of the street gave her a curious, and interested, glance, and she wheeled to her left and strode purposefully towards the more brightly lit King's Road, turning into the first café she came to.

The small room was filled with noisy chatter and smoke, but she managed to find an unoccupied table in a far corner. Her eyes roamed over the mainly student types who were cut from the same mould as Kerry and Joanna's friends, all anxious to state their own views but oblivious to those of their companions. Here and there she saw an older man or woman, from their garb probably artists, but only one pair of eyes gave her more than a casual glance, perhaps because their unusual colour piqued a momentary interest on her part, and their gazes locked until finally, embarrassed, she looked down at the coffee she had been neglecting and began hurriedly to sip it.

Her heart did a double-take when she saw, from the corner of her eye, that the man had risen and detached himself from the group he was with and was wending his way through the tables towards her. Wishing frantically that she had brought a book to pretend absorption in, Serena concentrated again on the milky coffee in her cup, her pulses hammering as she hoped devoutly he would go to the next table. But she was wedged into the corner, there wasn't a next table.

'Forgive me, but you seem a little lost in the corner,' he said in subtle question, his voice pleasant, cultured, without noticeable regional accent. 'Would you like to join us?'

Some of Serena's panic must have been revealed in the startled widening of her eyes, the sweep of colour into her face. She shook her head with more vigour than was necessary.

'I—no, thank you, I'm—not intending to stay long.' Under other circumstances she might have accepted. He had the long, lean physique and dark colouring that attracted her in a man, the darkness emphasised by the black casual trousers and black roll-necked sweater he wore. And there were those eyes, pale grey and holding a faintly amused glitter.

'Then do you mind if I join you before you rush off?' Without waiting for an answer, he pulled out the chair opposite and settled into it with an easy motion that made it difficult to take offence. It was only her own innate shyness that made her wish he would go away, back to his friends, who seemed scarcely to have noticed his departure.

'Let me get some more of this bilge they call coffee,' he raised a hand and the waitress appeared with miraculous speed. 'More for you?' he raised a black brow enquiringly and when Serena mutely shook her head, ordered for himself. His attention came back to Serena again, his eyes going over her face and hair and touching on the well-disguised contours of her figure under a jade sweater as loosely fitting as his own. 'Now, what's a beautiful girl doing in a place like this by herself, and looking very sad to boot?'

'I'm not sad,' she denied, hearing the tremor in her voice and suddenly irritated with her own gaucherie in face of his amused self-assurance. 'I can't get into my flat, so I decided to pass some time here.'

'You've lost your key?'

She stared at him for a moment, then forced a light laugh. 'Of course not. I share with two other art students, and we—er—take turns when we need privacy to—entertain. Understand?' she quoted Joanna so faithfully that her voice held the same strained patience as her flatmate's.

'I think so,' he said levelly, narrowing the grey eyes slightly. 'So you're an art student? At the Slade?'

Serena nodded, glancing up when the waitress deposited his coffee before him, conscious that his eyes were making another inspection of her face and what he could see of her figure. An unexpected thrill of excitement shot almost painfully through her; it was like a premonition of the fate destiny had in store for her—and it was completely without foundation, she told herself mockingly. She was attracted to this stranger because he was everything the men she had known so far were not. To begin with, he was at least ten years older than herself, and at thirty, with his rugged good looks, must have had more than his share of similarly experienced women. Studying him as he stirred his coffee, she reflected that the slight flatness across the bridge of his nose where it had obviously been broken at one time added to rather than detracted from his appeal. The small lines radiating from the unusual grey eyes spoke of a life lived to capacity, and she suddenly felt an overwhelming desire to be part of that life. Which was ridiculous, having known him for a total of ten minutes at most.

'You're very different from the average art student,' he looked up at her assessingly. 'I've never known one who looked like a forlorn mermaid with her eyes as green as the sea and hair as pale as moonlight on the ocean, a mouth carved from coral and a chin with the faintest suggestion of the rock underlying the waves.'

Lyrical words ... yet on his lips they weren't ridiculous. Perhaps he was a writer, a poet to whom words came easily. The thought was no sooner formed than she asked him if it was so, and he laughed deprecatingly.

'I'm afraid not,' he smiled lazily, 'though I had aspirations of that kind once, long ago. Fortunately, I discovered in time that while poetry might be satisfying to the soul, it would put little butter on my crust of bread.'

'So what do you do?' Serena pursued curiously.

He shrugged. 'I have a very dull job in the City which does little to feed my soul but ensures that the inner man is not neglected.'

'I couldn't do that,' Serena shook her head, her previous shyness completely gone. 'My work means so much to me, I think I'd die if I had to do something else.'

'Spoken like a true child of fortune,' he mocked, the grey eyes regarding her through half-lowered lids. 'You have the air of a privileged daughter of a wealthy father, am I right?'

Flustered, Serena's fingers toyed with the handle of her cup. 'Well, yes,' she admitted, 'I realise I'm fortunate in that I've never had to worry about finances, but even so ... I think even if my father had been poor I'd have found some way to do my art training. It means so much to me, you see,' she ended simply, looking up at him again and surprising his sardonic look. 'I really mean it.'

'I'm sure you do,' he dismissed her avowal carelessly, a softer light coming into his eyes as he went on, 'I'm almost afraid to ask your name. It would be anti-climatic to discover that it was Mabel or Ivy or something like that.'

'It's Serena. Serena Howard.'

'Perfect,' he smiled in surprised satisfaction, 'I couldn't have chosen better myself. And are you?'

'Am I what?' she frowned, puzzled.

'Serene.'

She laughed awkwardly. 'Our housekeeper in Bermuda would disagree, but yes, I'm fairly calm.'

'Bermuda?' The dark brows lifted again.

By the time Serena had explained her background the café, unnoticed by her until well after eleven, had emptied considerably. Feeling almost dazed, she looked around at the empty tables and reached for her handbag.

'I must go, I have an early class tomorrow,' she said, amazed at how the time had flown and how very relaxed she had felt in his company.

He rose as she did and laid light fingers on her elbow as they left the café. 'I'll walk you home,' he said in a voice that brooked no argument, and Serena made no objection. Never in her life had she been so relaxed with a man not her father, and she wanted to prolong this meeting to the last possible moment. That came all too soon, since the café was only a short distance from the flat.

'Well,' she looked up at him, noticing that the grey eyes were shaded in the light cast from the street lamp immediately outside the two-storey house where she lived, 'this is it. Thank you for—passing the waiting time so pleasantly for me.'

'The pleasure was mine.' Her nerve ends contracted when he lifted her hand and pressed the back of her fingers to his lips. 'May I see you again?'

'I'd like that,' she admitted honestly. 'We're—having a party here on Saturday evening, could you manage that?'

'Unfortunately no. I have a little place in the country, and I spend most weekends there. Partly to get away from the city, but mostly to catch up on paperwork I don't get round to dealing with during the week. How would this coming Friday suit you? We can drive downriver and find a private spot to have dinner.'

'That would be lovely. What time?'

The time had been arranged and she was already

halfway to the house entrance when she turned and called softly after him. 'You didn't tell me your name.'

'It's Benedict,' his voice carried easily on the night air, 'Benedict Ramsey.'

He was the answer to her prayer for a man to share her blindingly passionate love affair; she didn't have to sleep with him to know that they would be perfect for each other. From the first time he had taken her in his arms to kiss her, she knew that.

It was after that first dinner, driving back from the secluded riverside hotel where they had been able to talk and begin to know each other in absolute privacy, that Benedict had pulled off into the quiet darkness of a leafy lane and turned to her, his hands infinitely gentle as they cupped her face then traced its outlines. She shivered when his thumb brushed tenderly across the carved fullness of her lower lip, and trembled when at last his mouth replaced it, continuing the slow and shakingly sensuous movement. It was as if she had never been kissed before, and certainly she had never experienced the slow, almost painful, sensations that flowed through her and concentrated like a palpable thing at the pit of her stomach.

'Beautiful mermaid,' Benedict's voice came muffled from the sloping join of her neck and body, and she fought off an initial shyness when his fingers found and released the zipper of her dress and then the fastening of her bra and stroked the eager fullness of her breasts.

She was helpless to prevent the low moan that

welled up from her throat, and the sound had an immediate effect on Benedict. With a savagery that was almost frightening, his mouth claimed hers again and parted her lips with easy mastery, provoking a dizzy spiralling of her senses that left her clinging desperately to the muscular line of his shoulders, her eyes closing as her hands groped instinctively for the heated warmth of his neck and up to the cooler thickness of hair that felt silky smooth on her fingertips.

Later, she felt guilt that it had been Benedict who pulled away, set her from him and stared into the drugged glaze of her eyes. But then, she knew only the sharp disappointment of rejection.

'Don't stop,' she whispered, her fingers lightly tracing the taut line of his jaw. 'Please.'

To her surprise, his mouth twisted into a wry smile. 'You've obviously never tried making love in a car before. I don't want this,' he gestured towards the dark interior, 'the first time. You deserve more than that, mermaid.'

Serena was so moved with the gratitude that rushed through her that she slid over to her side of the car and rearranged her clothing without demur. Not only was he the sexiest man she had ever met, he was sensitive too. She had no illusions about being the first for him; a man of thirty obviously hadn't lived as a celibate in his mature years. That fact had given him the experienced knowledge that for her this would be the first time. He wanted it to be something special for her, not an awkward assignation at the rear of a car.

Serena ran the gamut of emotions during the next weeks, from dizzy ecstasy to the depths of despair. Ecstasy when Benedict made it obvious that he wanted to be with her, casting an aura of romance round their meetings, whether it was to wander round the art galleries hand in hand or to dine in the delightfully intimate restaurants he constantly found; despair when the grand passion she had envisioned got no further off the ground than it had that first night. It was almost insulting when, time after time, he was the one to call a halt to the lovemaking that drove her roused senses to the point where even the back seat of his small car would have provided a welcome release.

But Benedict was adamant. 'This isn't what I want for us,' he repeated huskily, endlessly.

'What *do* you want for us?' Serena finally asked tersely, staring out at yet another darkened country lane. 'You think I'm too young for you, don't you?'

He sighed. 'There is quite a gap between our ages,' he conceded, 'but it's not that. Oh God, Serena, you deserve better than a furtive coupling in the back of a car,' he said tautly, his fist striking an angry motion against the wheel.

'Then take me with you to your country place,' she cried with wanton disregard. 'I—won't make demands on you, if that's what you're thinking,' she went on more quietly. 'I've no more intention of becoming a dreary housewife than you have of making me one. I—just want you to be mine for now.' Her lips, her fingers, her legs all trembled with the lie. She had quickly realised that she wanted him to be the first, last and only love of her life. But conventional visions of rose-covered cottages and children tumbling round him weren't Benedict's scene ... now. Surely he would see it differently when they at last shed the protective layers each had erected against the other.

'I share the cottage with a writer friend,' he said in the remote voice she had come to know, 'but I'll see what I can do.'

Serena loved Chisholm Cottage on sight. Light purple wisteria draped the slightly sagging entrance porch and flowers that had once been cultivated rioted uncaringly in the jaggedly hedged front garden. A winding flagstone path led to the front entrance of the low-slung plaster cottage, and blood-red peonies drooped on their stalks like wounded soldiers bowed and bloody at either side of the entrance.

'It's lovely!' she exclaimed involuntarily, turning to Benedict with a brilliant smile. 'How can you ever bear to leave it?'

'It's a far cry from the gardens of Bermuda and a clear turquoise sea,' he returned drily. 'How could you bear to leave that?'

She shrugged and turned away, too nervous suddenly to contemplate what this weekend in the country implied. It was one thing to indulge in reckless daydreams, quite another to know their realisation. 'This could almost be Bermuda,' she mused aloud. 'Morning glories just like those,' she indicated the wide blue blossoms decorating an arch that led round the side of the cottage, 'grow almost everywhere there. And roses like those bloom all year round in Bermuda, though I've noticed they have a short season here ...' Her back to Benedict, she wasn't aware of his approach until his hands fell on her shoulders and spun her round to face him.

'Stop it, Serena! You didn't come down here to make a comparative inventory of the garden, any more than I came to contemplate the wonders of bucolic contentment.' Her eyes followed the curt jerk of his head to the low hedge bordering the cottage property, beyond which white-faced cows ruminated thoughtfully as their offspring nudged eagerly at swollen udders. Wishing suddenly that she possessed a modicum of the sophistication either of her flatmates would have displayed under similar circumstances, Serena brought her gaze back to the man whose eyes burned with a steely intensity into hers.

This was the moment she had longed for, waited for, so why did she so urgently feel the need to flee, to run for her life? If only Benedict loved her the way she loved him, she thought despairingly, her body traitorous to the thought when he reached out and drew her to the strong arc of his body. His mouth when he kissed her held the warmth of the sun that slanted its way down towards the west, and as her lips opened to the pressure of his the question seemed unimportant.

As if it was preordained, Benedict bent and scooped her up into his arms, bearing her so swiftly into the low-ceilinged cottage that she saw nothing of the lower floor. There was only the faint billowing of creamy muslin curtains at the pair of dormer windows flanking the high-lofted bed, the angled walls that rose haphazardly to meet the narrow strip of white ceiling, the scent of early summer flowers drifting through the open windows.

It was a day of enchantment, a cottage of enchantment, a man who exuded enchantment from every pore. Serena's senses swam, cleared, misted over again. Her arms reached up in wordless entreaty and Benedict hesitated only for a moment before coming into them, the mattress bending under his weight as he half-stretched beside her. His eyes were like opaque pools in a pale grey sea as he said huskily, 'You're sure?'

She nodded, and he bent to kiss her gently, almost reverently, on cheeks, brow, ears, seeming to carefully avoid the trembling fullness of her lips until her hands lifted from his shoulders and rose to cup the tensed leanness of his jaws. 'Love me, Benedict,' she whispered huskily, drawing his mouth down to the readiness of her own, feeling her own response quicken when he brushed lightly with his mouth across hers, then slid his hands under her to draw her up to the sudden abrasive demand of his kiss. For a moment she held back, a last nod to the proprieties that had bound her all her life.

After that, there was no holding back, no shrinking from the unfamiliar sensations Benedict evoked with his lips, his hands. Her skin felt like satin, velvet, as his hands roved over the highs and lows of the body he had made naked. Brief embarrassment flared in her eyes when the rough knit of Benedict's blue sweater brushed abrasively over her rounded breasts, making her tinglingly aware that he was still fully dressed; then embarrassment was replaced with shivery excitement when, as if reading her mind, he murmured huskily, 'Now you undress me.'

Her fingers trembled so much that he had to help her with the leather belt securing his tight-fitting jeans, and he stood to remove them completely. Serena wanted to close her eyes, turn her head away on the down-soft pillow, anything

rather than stare unashamedly at the first man she
had seen completely uncovered. But her gaze
refused to follow her instinct, wandering in
wonder from sparsely fleshed shoulders to tautly
muscled chest covered lightly with the springing
roughness of dark hair that narrowed to a point
just above the flat stomach. Powerful thighs, his
maleness, the sinewy calves were as much as she
could see, but she was stunned by the sheer beauty
of his masculine perfection.

He stretched out beside her on his side, arcing
an arm above her head on the pillow, and said,
sounding faintly amused, 'You look as if you've
never seen a naked man before.'

'I—haven't reached life classes in art school yet,'
she said innocently, but he must have thought she
was joking because his smile reached up to his
eyes, crinkling the skin around them. Not much
later she knew that he *had* thought her words a
joke, but at that moment all her senses were aware
of was the potent warmth of his hard flesh beside
her, the slow bend of his head for his mouth to
reach hers and tantalise her lips with soft light
kisses that roused her more surely than if he had
fallen on her in an attack of wild passion.

It was she who murmured impatiently and
twined her arms round his neck to draw him
closer, her lips parting to deepen the kiss to the
intimacy she had known before with him. But still
he held back, seeming content to bring her to the
peak of arousal with hands that caressed, stroked,
pressured until her skin prickled with the fire
building deep within her straining body. When his
lips and tongue followed his hands to her breasts
to lave their hardened peaks she groaned with the

pleasure he was inciting in her and reached with her hands to pleasure him in the same way. Her touch was unsure, inept, but Benedict's sharp hiss of breath told her that she had reached the same sensual core as he had found in her. He came over her, his mouth devouring as it claimed hers with all the passion she had expected from his first kiss.

Breath screamed for release in her lungs, expelling when he at last lifted his mouth from hers in a half-sobbing wail. 'Benedict . . . oh, Benedict, I love you!' The words seemed to hang in the air of the sunwarmed cottage bedroom, replaced moments later by the cry of pain torn from her throat as Benedict took her forcefully with a piercing shaft of agony that left her breathless. It was a momentary thing, and pain was forgotten in the surge of ecstasy that filled her and arched her body to meet Benedict's.

She lay with her eyes closed when Benedict rolled away, exhausted in a strange new way, euphorically content in another. Was this how Kerry, Joanna, felt when they had made love with their varied partners? No, it couldn't be . . . she would never want anyone but Benedict for her lover, couldn't bear the thought of another man taking his place in her bed. And that meant . . .

She felt the bed's depression when Benedict moved and sat up and forced her lethargic eyelids open to see him sitting at the edge of the bed, his feet on the floor, his hands pressed to his eyes.

'Benedict, what is it?' Alarmed, she sat up and worked her way forward until she could touch his shoulder. Surely she hadn't been *that* inept! But as he took his hands from his eyes and let them drop between his knees, she saw anger, not disappointment, etching his mouth with bitter lines.

'Why the hell didn't you tell me?' he said harshly, his eyes cold as the Atlantic winds that sometimes swept Bermuda.

'T-tell you what?' she stammered, her voice rising almost to shrillness.

'That you're a—that you were,' he corrected acidly, 'a virgin?'

Serena moved back, less worried now that she knew the reason for his sudden change of face, though she drew the abandoned sheet up to cover her nakedness in face of the hostile look he was giving her.

'You didn't ask me,' she flared in brief irritation which died almost as soon as it arose. Men— experienced men—for some reason didn't like to think they had been responsible for the deflowering of a virgin; it probably had origins far back in history when men were chivalrous and women one of two types ... good or bad. Archaic thinking, but Benedict obviously still allowed it credence.

'For God's sake, why would I ask you?' He ran a shaking hand through his hair. 'You're an art student, you should know the score. The first time we met,' he said heavily, 'you told me you and your flatmates take turns at entertaining in privacy.'

Serena stared at him, shocked. That much was true—hadn't she gone into the café that night with the sole purpose of passing time until ... But surely if he had come to love her since he must have known that she could never conduct a love affair under those circumstances, her two flatmates at least aware that she had only one reason for privacy when she brought a man there. Hurt deeper than any she had known spread like pangs of pain inside her, then came out distilled as anger.

'If it's your precious bachelorhood you're worried about, you can forget it,' she snapped, vaulting from the bed and savagely drawing on the clothes he had deprived her of so slickly. 'Unlike you, I don't adhere to archaic rules that say if you sleep with a virgin you marry her. I've already told you that my career is more important to me than any man, even you, could be!' Her jeans zipper buzzed noisily as she jerked it up, then snatched her boat-necked green top from the floor near his feet and slid it over her head. Taking a comb from her abandoned bag, she stared at herself furiously in the faded revolving mirror of an ancient dresser as she tugged some semblance of order into her tangled fair hair.

'Serena, you don't understand,' he began wearily, stepping into his jeans and standing to fasten them at his narrow waist.

'I understand very well,' blazed Serena, twirling rapidly on her heels to face him, her eyes forbiddingly contemptuous. 'You expected a nice, uncomplicated, dirty weekend in a picture cottage with a sexy, maybe kinky, art student. Well,' she demanded blisteringly, 'isn't that exactly what you got? You can tell all your friends that, wow, you slept with a virgin when they ask what you did at the weekend!'

'Stop it, Serena.' Benedict, still clothed only in the nether regions, stepped across and shook her by the shoulders until her hair bounced like molten silver. The anger in his grey eyes lessened and disappeared as she stared angrily into them. 'Now isn't the time,' he shook his head, then turned away, his hands dropping from her shoulders to leave her miserably aware of how much she would miss the touch of his lean hard flesh on hers. 'I'll drive you back to London,' he said quietly.

Serena wished she could spurn the lukewarm offer, but she had no idea if there was a telephone in the cottage, let alone a nearby train that would take her back to the city. She waited outside while he dressed and locked up the cottage for his writer friend. Perhaps, she thought in grim amusement, his friend could bring into his writings the amazing phenomenon of a twenty-year-old art student virgin—ex-virgin, she reminded herself bleakly as she got silently into the car beside the morose-looking Benedict.

The journey, undertaken in silence, seemed to take twice as long as the trip down to the cottage. It wasn't far from the city, situated as it was on the southern borders of Essex, but the wheels couldn't move fast enough for Serena. She remembered gratefully that Joanna had left on Thursday for a long weekend in Paris, and that Kerry was spending one of her rare weekends with her family. The flat would be hers to weep the tears that hovered brilliantly at the back of her eyes—tears she was determined Benedict wouldn't see. It would really crown his chauvinistic toss in the covers to see that she wept for him.

For him—or for herself? The thought was still uppermost in her mind when she let herself into the apartment, the emptiness within herself echoed in the small, silent rooms. Benedict! . . . oh God, Benedict . . . the tears welled, profuse after being confined so long, and Serena stumbled to the tiny room that was hers at the rear of the flat and threw herself on the narrow bed, giving vent to the raw emotions that clawed with knifelike sharpness inside her. Could anything not physical hurt this much? She wanted to flee, run back to Bermuda and her bluff, hearty father ... but she couldn't even do that. Charles would never understand a passion so strong that she would sacrifice her precious virginity to it. In that sense, he and Benedict were close in their thinking. Virgins were for marrying, experienced women were for jaded male appetites. She had always, it seemed, known about the women who floated on the periphery of Charles' life, but he had never brought them home to Windfair. No other woman had aspired to fill her mother's shoes, and since Serena adored her father in a possessive way, this state of status quo suited her admirably.

She turned on her back and stared at the flyspecked ceiling. Love had come and gone so quickly in her life she had scarcely appreciated its presence. Despite Benedict's terse comment that he would be in touch, she knew she would never see him again. Virgins were bad news to single men.

Yet she did see him again. On the Friday evening following, her twenty-first birthday as it happened, Joanna came with her languid stride into the untidy living room towing a Benedict whose hard-set jaw might never have heard of tenderness, compassion. Serena scrambled to her feet from the low-slung couch strewn with the art prints she had been studying, her eyes reflecting the amazement she felt at seeing Benedict's tall, commanding figure in the cluttered disorder of the living room.

'A gentleman caller for you, ma'am,' Joanna assumed her facetious maidservant routine, her eyes rolling appreciatively over Benedict's well-set figure in a dark grey formal suit that deepened the colour of his eyes. 'The kitchen staff will be very grateful for the leftovers,' Joanna quipped as she bobbed a half-curtsy in Serena's direction and went to the door with swinging hips, turning back there to say reproachfully, 'I suppose this means, madam, that the birthday celebrations the staff have slaved over for a whole week are obsolete now?'

'Feed the peasants with it,' Serena automatically fell in with her flatmate's twisted sense of humour, her eyes sobering as they came back to Benedict, who stood slightly dazedly at the centre of the room. 'I'm sorry,' she apologised in a perfunctory way, 'Joanna should have studied drama rather than art.' She waved a hand in the air as if to summon a fully equipped bar. 'May I offer you something to drink?'

'As long as she hasn't studied *Macbeth* too closely,' he rose to the occasion, albeit sombrely, 'I'd like a glass of wine if you have it.'

'I'd stick to the white if I were you,' she advised darkly, amazed and pleased by her own poise as she moved to the door. 'Joanna's a little heavy-handed on the toad's feet she considers necessary to make a full-bodied red.'

'Then the white, by all means.'

The bright social veneer she had assumed for Benedict's unexpected presence dropped from her the moment she passed through the door that led to the small galley-type kitchen, now as ever looking as if a bomb had torn its devastation through it. Joanna's eyes rolled expressively as she poured the remains of a sadly depleted bottle into the glass Serena unearthed at the back of the cupboard.

'Why so glum, when a dish like that awaits you in the living room?' she queried curiously.

'I'm not glum. I just don't want to see him any more, that's all.'

'The child must have a fever,' Joanna said despairingly, her hand testing the heat of Serena's brow. Then something she saw in the sea-green eyes sobered her to seriousness. 'You're in love with him, infant, aren't you?'

Serena nodded, seeing no need to preserve the privacy she had sensed Benedict demanded in their relationship. Tears rose and were rapidly blinked away. She couldn't bear commiseration over a love affair from Joanna of all people. Love and let love was her policy, and let the chips fall where they may.

'But I can handle it,' Serena assured her with a confidence that failed her as soon as she carried the tulip-shaped glass into the living room and handed it to Benedict. He was still standing in the middle of the room, his expression one of stunned disdain as he glanced at the debris scattered liberally on floor and chairs and sofa.

Embarrassed warmth put faint colour into Serena's pale cheeks and she started forward to make a hasty clear-up of the mess, then stopped, confining her efforts to the best of the armchairs, clearing a spot for him to sit. Her mouth was pressed tightly together; she certainly hadn't asked him to come here, and if the flat offended him he would just have to leave again.

'You can sit there,' she waved an ungracious hand towards the armchair and returned to her own seat on the sofa, occupying her trembling hands by shuffling together the art prints she had been studying.

'Thanks, I prefer to stand.'

She shrugged, wishing there had been enough wine to fill a glass for herself. The room was suffocatingly small with him in it, and she was excruciatingly aware of every small detail about him. She had never seen him so grandly dressed; the dark grey suit seemed tailored to his tall, lean figure and reflected its darker grey to his eyes. His hair had lost its casually ruffled look and was neatly brushed back from his face, which was also the face of a stranger. Serena wished acutely that she had made more effort with her appearance, but she had been listlessly uninterested these past few days. That much was patently obvious to less discerning eyes than Benedict's ... her hair was scraped back from a face devoid of make-up of any kind, the shapeless sweater top was one she reserved for her sporadic efforts to tidy the flat, and her jeans were the oldest, most faded ones she possessed.

'Is it true?'

She jumped when Benedict spoke, then gave him a tight upward glance. 'Is what true?'

'That it's your birthday today.'

'I can't imagine what significance that can possibly have for you,' she returned coolly. She noted that he hadn't touched the wine in his glass, and wondered sardonically as she returned her sightless attention to the prints if he suspected the glass might not be quite clean. In the suit and tie and crisply laundered white shirt he looked more like a stockbroker than a humble City worker hunched over a desk all day.

'I must talk to you, Serena,' he said in a low, intense voice, probably afraid that Joanna would hear him in the kitchen. 'It's obvious we can't talk here, so will you come out and have dinner with me?'

'My friends are giving a party for me, so I'm afraid that's impossible. In any case——'

Joanna's timing couldn't have been worse. Evidently overhearing Benedict's dinner invitation, she came and leaned casually on the door frame and drawled, 'Of course you must go and have dinner, you know nothing's going to start around here until ten or so.' Her gaze went round the debris-filled room and she added wryly, 'It will take me that long to clear a few passageways in this lot anyway, if Kerry deigns not to show up until things are underway, as she's been known to do.'

'I'm not dressed to go out to dinner,' Serena gritted meaningly, 'and I was about to start cleaning up in here.'

'Nonsense,' her friend dismissed crisply, pointing out that she was going to have to change anyway, and she wouldn't hear of her working on her birthday. 'I'll entertain your friend while you're getting ready,' she ended, smiling as she advanced into the room, and Serena's eyes involuntarily met Benedict's, wondering if he was, like her, recalling the connotation of the word 'entertain' in this apartment. But there was no change in his level gaze. 'Let me see if I can find you something a little more palatable than that,' Joanna began again, ignoring Serena as she took the glass from Benedict's hand. 'Whisky all right?'

Amazed, Serena got up and followed her into the kitchen. 'What do you mean, whisky?' she demanded in a fierce whisper. 'You know we never have anything but wine in the flat.'

Joanna reached up for a squat tumbler, winking as she turned back. 'I always keep some for emergencies and for men like your Benedict who obviously appreciates the finer things in life.'

'He's not my Benedict!' Serena gritted, bringing Joanna's eyes round to look at her speculatively.

'To be frank, I wouldn't have thought you were at all his type, easier to imagine him with some super-glamorous bitch woman. But don't look bountiful fate in the teeth, darling, enjoy while you can.'

She left the kitchen and went with her unhurried gait along the short passageway to her bedroom where, presumably, she secreted the whisky bottle. Other than make a scene, Serena had no choice but to stamp furiously into her own tiny room and slide hangers noisily along the rail that held her clothes in a curtained alcove. She hadn't told her flatmates about the abortive weekend in Essex, knowing she couldn't bear their pity or possible amusement. If she made a fuss now over a simple dinner invitation from a man as attractive as Benedict, the whole sick story would have to come out.

More as self-defence than in a wish to please her escort, Serena pulled out a plain black dress ... plain but with a superb cut that spoke of expense, of sophistication, poise. Most of all, it lent her a maturity she was badly in need of where Benedict was concerned. Under the shower, and later as she blow-dried her hair, she realised she was frighteningly unsure of what her attitude should be towards him. Cool, as she had been in the living room minutes ago? Blasé about the whole thing? Best stick to cool, she decided, sliding the black dress over her head and adjusting its fit to her bust, waist and slender hips and surveying herself in the small dressing-table mirror where she had to view herself piecemeal. She had applied make-up more liberally than usual to counteract the pallid state of her cheeks, and stroked pale grey shadow on her lids, the colour somehow intensifying the green of her eyes. A touch of mascara to her lashes and a light pencilling of brows and upper lid helped in her struggle for poise, and the light coppertone lipstick struck just the right note for her purposes. Her hair she left loose to her shoulders; there wasn't time to arrange it in the sophisticated chignon she would have preferred.

A final dab of the expensive perfume she seldom used left her with nothing more to do. Too strung up to feel ridiculous, she forced a smile on her lips and noted its effects in the mirror. Whoever had written that to appear happy one had only to smile at one's reflection in a mirror must have been out of his or her mind!

CHAPTER THREE

'FOR a gal who wasn't interested in going out to dinner with this man,' Joanna said drily as she stood in the doorway to Serena's room, 'you've taken a lot of trouble to make your point.'

Serena essayed a smile, knowing it was no more effective than the one she had practised in the mirror. 'Aren't I entitled to dress up a bit on my birthday?' she said defensively.

'No contest there, but I think I'd better send out some smoke signals to advise the other party members that they'll feel like Cinderella after midnight if they come in their usual attire.'

'Don't be silly, I'll change as soon as I get back.' In an access of uncertainty, Serena looked appealingly at Joanna. 'Are you sure I look all right?'

'Let me just say this,' Joanna said, duly solemn, 'the cream of filmdom would give their Swiss chalets and Beverly Hills mansions to look as you and your Benedict look tonight.'

'You're ridiculous,' Serene smiled genuinely at last, 'but I'm glad you said it.'

The smile still lingered in her sea-green eyes when she stepped into the untidy living room where Benedict had at last subsided into a chair. In a strange way she felt like Serena Howard of Windfair on her way to a social occasion in her native Bermuda. Her partners then had gazed at her in bemused appreciation, much as Benedict now did as he got slowly to his feet.

'You look beautiful,' he said in a husky voice that reverberated against her spine and sent remembered shafts of the last time he had spoken that way piercing through her. Light, she reminded herself, keep it cool and light.

'Thank you. I'm sorry if I kept you waiting too long.'

He seemed about to say something, but checked himself before moving across to take her elbow. 'Shall we go?'

The car he was driving tonight was so much larger, more luxurious, than the small one she was used to that she turned puzzled eyes on him as he slid into the driving seat beside her and turned the ignition key.

'Is this yours?' she asked bluntly, knowing as she posed the question that the pure leather-upholstered car must be his, his movements were too familiarly efficient to suppose otherwise.

'Yes.'

'I—didn't know you had more than one car.' She was beginning to suspect, her heart beginning to beat in a double-time rhythm, that there was more, a lot more, that she didn't know about Benedict Ramsey. The thought shocked her. She had never envisioned him as anything but what he appeared ... a man bored with his job in the labyrinthine depths of the City, turning for light relief to the more carefree creative scene in Chelsea. But suppose he was one of those kinky rich men she'd read about, men who escaped the pressures of corporate life by merging into the no-questions-asked artistic colony?

Even to her jaundiced mind the idea of Benedict living a double life was ludicrous. So he had more

than one car ... many people ran two cars, one
economical, the other reserved for special occasions
when a show of status seemed necessary. That
started another train of thought, one she nipped
smartly in the bud. She could go on endlessly
speculating about the life he had told her little
about, and she would still be left with the bare
facts. She had fallen in love with him, but his
intentions were no more serious than a rough-and-
tumble in a cottage bedroom. The fault was hers,
not his.

'Where are we going?' She moistened her lips
with her tongue before voicing the question,
knowing she would hate it if she sounded at all
strained, parched.

His head turned from the half-empty street ahead,
his eyes flicking down over the black dress and
cobwebby stole she had draped across her
shoulders. 'Francesco's seems more appropriate
than anywhere else,' he said drily, naming the
newest of London's "in" restaurants. 'I'll see if
they have a table for us.'

The possibility seemed remote when they stood
at the entrance to the dining room minutes later
and surveyed the crowded scene, but miraculously
the head waiter beckoned them to a table for two
adjacent to the small dance floor. Serena was
conscious of female eyes covertly appraising
Benedict's confident figure, totally unconscious of
the male eyes that ran appreciatively over her and
found her desirable.

'Good God!' a young man in evening dress got
to his feet as Benedict and Serena passed the table
for four, 'is it you, Serena?'

She paused and took a closer look, then her face

broke out into a belated smile. 'Matthew! What are you doing here?'

'The same as you, I presume,' he tossed back, grinning. 'Why don't you and your friend join us?' His smile faded slightly when his eyes shifted to Benedict's icily remote stare. 'We can easily pull up another two chairs, and we haven't ordered yet, so we can all eat together.'

Serena's eyes shone with a not uncalculated pleasure as she turned to Benedict. 'This is Matthew Prentiss from Bermuda,' she explained. 'Matthew, this is Benedict Ramsey.'

Two waiters bearing laden trays attempted to pass them, and Serena sidestepped towards Matthew's table and found herself deposited suddenly in his chair.

'Come on, Benedict, let's find ourselves a couple of seats,' Matthew urged gleefully, seemingly unaware of Benedict's reluctance to join the party of four.

'I think not, if you don't mind,' he said stiffly, his hand imperative on Serena's shoulder. 'Serena and I are—celebrating something special and we'd like to be alone.'

Matthew's eyes took on a deeper sparkle. 'You're getting married, Serena?' he guessed, not questioning his conclusion. 'Then of course you want to be alone.' He smiled at Benedict as he stretched out his hand. 'Congratulations! A lot of hearts will shrivel up and die in Bermuda tonight. Our Serena has a lot of strings to her bow.'

'I don't doubt it,' Benedict returned equably, though he seemed distracted as he laid light fingers on her elbow and led her to the table originally meant for them. 'This wasn't the best choice for a quiet talk,' he observed irritably as he seated himself opposite her. A waiter appeared instantly at his side. 'What would you like to drink?'

'Daiquiri, please.' Something told her that this evening would demand more than the usual white wine. Already a churning was beginning in her stomach. Why hadn't Benedict made the situation clear to Matthew, that it wasn't a coming marriage they were celebrating, but her birthday? Her eyes took on a fixed stare as she looked across at Benedict, his dark lashes lowered as he perused the huge red leather menu. Or was that the real reason for this expensive splurge, for his broody brow, his contained quietness? Did he intend asking her tonight to marry him?

A corner of her mouth trembled, but not with happiness. Could he really understand her so little that he thought she would jump at the chance to marry the man who had taken her virginity and felt guilty about it? How wrong, how very wrong he was, not just for her but for himself. To live a life of obligation, without love to leaven it, would be purgatory for him too.

Their drinks arrived, and the Scotch gleamed gold against the darker outline of his fingers as Benedict lifted the glass and took a thirsty swallow before looking unguardedly contrite. 'Sorry,' he apologised softly, 'we ought to have toasted the reaching of your majority.'

'I reached that three years ago, according to current thinking,' she retorted crisply, the words a primed barb aimed for all his out-of-date convictions. That they had hit home was evident in the sudden tightening of his mouth as he raised his glass.

'Nevertheless, I'd like to wish you long life and—the kind of happiness you truly deserve.'

Serena's throat constricted suddenly at the bittersweet expression in his eyes, as if he were at the same time saying goodbye to his own future happiness. She wanted to say—no, scream—that she had no intention of accepting his proposal of marriage, but all that came out was a strangled, 'Would you order for me? I have to . . .'

She fled, threading her way through the dining room, careful to avoid Matthew's table, knowing she would be no more capable of speaking logically to him than she could to Benedict. The cloakroom was blessedly empty and she slumped into one of the two upholstered seats beside the sink-lined vanity. It was a cowardly act, to run away from the first real emotional challenge she had known, she chided herself. Charles, her father, would have said, 'Face up to it, my darling, no matter how painful. You might learn something from the experience.'

But this wasn't a tennis game where she'd been outmatched by a superior player, a gymkhana where she'd been in competition with older, more experienced riders. This was something that affected every fibre of her being, the deep emotional part where she lived. She couldn't bear to think of her life without Benedict in it, yet she could never marry him knowing that he took her into his life from a sense of obligation, not love. He hadn't once mentioned love . . . oh, there had been muttered phrases that day in the cottage, but never 'I love you'. A tear trickled softly down her cheek, making her aware that she was crying and that she must repair her make-up and get back to the table.

Voices approaching the ladies' room when she was halfway out of the chair made her dart like a criminal into one of the cubicles and shoot home the bolt. She was in no mood to explain the reason for her tears to curious strangers. She stood with her back to the steel door as the two women used the adjoining cubicles, then met again at the mirrored vanity. They sounded to be in their late twenties or early thirties. Sophisticatedly bored, by the start of their conversation.

'I don't know why Ronnie likes this place so much,' said the first voice in an upper-class drawl. 'Dreary food, dreary atmosphere, dreary people.'

'Oh, I don't know about that,' the other woman inserted, her words muffled as she applied lipstick, 'didn't I see Benedict Ramsey with a delectable blonde who might be a film star?'

The first woman laughed unpleasantly. 'Film star she may be, but she's far too young to tangle with the likes of Caroline Ramsey. Possessive wife is putting it mildly!'

Serena's hands clenched into white knuckled fists as the conversation drifted over to her. Wife . . . wife . . . wife. Benedict had a wife.

'. . . doesn't he divorce her?' the voice came over the roaring in Serena's ears.

A derisive laugh came before, 'Whatever else he may be, Benedict Ramsey isn't stupid. Sir Harold Cranston's shoes have been stretched to accommodate his son-in-law's feet. Everybody knows that the Chairmanship of the bank will go to Benedict Ramsey when the old man steps down. Oh no, my dear, Ramsey will never divorce her, for all her shortcomings . . . he's a man with an eye to his future. It's rather a shame, though, about the . . .'

The voices faded into nothing as the women left the ladies' room, but moments, minutes ticked by as Serena stood frozen against the cubicle door. Oh God, he was *married* . . . married to a woman called Caroline . . . a woman obviously able to secure his future as Chairman of the bank. Dry rasping sobs wracked Serena's throat as she pressed her head back against the cold steel of the door. What an idiot she had been! Like spent leaves falling to the ground in a preordained pattern, facts fell into place with deadly accuracy.

Benedict hadn't chosen those out-of-the-way character restaurants for the aura of romance they offered. He had chosen them because none of his, or his wife's, acquaintances were likely to see them there. Or at the art galleries they had wandered round hand in hand . . . those were spacious enough for him to see them far in advance and drop the intimate clasp of her fingers. Her fists pounded on the cold metal of the door. Idiot, idiot, idiot echoed with each blow. Damn him . . . damn him for his lies, for his use of the attraction he had for many women, herself included.

'Is there a Serena Howard in here?' a tentative female voice intruded into her stormy thoughts, and she unlatched the door.

'I'm Serena Howard,' she said tautly to the anxious matronly figure hesitating just inside the outer door.

'Oh . . . well, there's a man outside and he asked me to . . .'

'I'll talk to him, thank you.' Serena swept by her in sudden resolve, uncaring about her tear-smudged cheeks or the mascara that must have run at least a little. She wanted to hear the truth from Benedict's lips, and then it would be over. The affair of passion she had foolishly dreamed about and even more foolishly turned into a romance of love everlasting.

If she hadn't known better, the Benedict who hovered close to the cloakroom door might have been any man lovingly concerned for the woman in his life.

'What the hell happened to you?' he demanded aggressively, his lean fingers gouging the thin layer of flesh covering her shoulders. 'I thought you must have left . . .'

'That's exactly what I'm going to do,' she returned sweetly, 'as soon as I've told you exactly what I think you, Benedict Ramsey, husband of Caroline who's very, very possessive, which forces you to conduct your sexual affairs far from the madding crowd. Shall I go on?'

Even without the dazed shake of his head she couldn't have continued. Not when his face had taken on the grey colour of illness, his eyes the glitter of fever.

'How long have you known?' he asked hoarsely.

'Five—ten minutes. One hears all sorts of titillating gossip in the ladies' room.'

'For God's sake, Serena,' he gritted in a low tone that might have been calculated not to draw the attention of restaurant patrons milling in the entrance, 'that's exactly what I brought you here to tell you tonight. That however much I want to, I can't marry you.'

'That was very brave of you, Benedict,' she said with solemn sarcasm. 'After all, I might have gone to your father-in-law, the Chairman of the bank where you work, and told him that you'd seduced me. That would have dulled the polish on the shoes you expect to fill, wouldn't it? Or are your extra-marital affairs too commonplace to merit attention?'

His mouth, the mouth that had acted in such close concert with his hands in arousing her to sexual excitement, twisted into a bitter, sardonic line. 'The cloakroom gossips did their work well, didn't they? Now perhaps you'll be fair enough to hear the other side of it.'

'Is there another side to a man who cheats on his wife but stays with her because—oh God, because her father can assure a plushy future for him?' Her voice thick with emotion, with the loathing she felt for him at that moment, she said before turning away, 'You and your kind make me sick, Benedict Ramsey, and I hope I never see you again!'

Benedict made no attempt to follow her as she redeemed her stole from the determinedly smiling girl who manned the coat-check near the outer doors, nor as she stood uncertainly on the flight of steps leading down to the street from the restaurant. When an expressionless doorman asked, 'Taxi, madam?' she nodded without speaking and got into the taxi he gestured to at the head of several waiting for discharging patrons of the restaurant. Still Benedict didn't come, and she didn't know if she was relieved or sorry as she sat back in the shadowy depths of the taxi after giving the driver her address.

Tears welled painfully into her throat and eyes, but she willed them away. Her father's hearty voice echoed in her mind. 'Face it and learn something from the experience.' She had certainly done that. No man would ever again reach the soft, vulnerable core she had opened so willingly to Benedict. The perfect love she had girlishly envisaged had no reality in the everyday world. She had been scalded by the heat; in future she would stay out of that particular kitchen.

She had come out without money, and she said to the driver as he drew up to the kerb outside her flat, 'Would you mind waiting while I fetch the fare? I—wasn't expecting to . . .'

'That's all right, miss,' he returned tolerantly, having observed her facially reflected mental struggles through the rear-view mirror, 'as long as you're quick about it.'

'Thank you.' Serena slid across to the kerb-side door and let herself out of the taxi. Some sixth sense told her something was amiss as she climbed the front steps, but it was only as she went into the upper flat that she realised what it was. The party in honour of her birthday hadn't yet got under way. Which wasn't surprising, considering it was nowhere near the ten o'clock witching hour Joanna had mentioned.

Still there was an unearthly and unfamiliar quietness in the apartment, and she stared curiously at Kerry and Joanna, who sat as if waiting for the party to begin at either side of the now-tidy living room.

'I have to get some money for the taxi driver,' Serena said into the silence, and was faintly shocked to hear a muffled sob coming from Kerry. 'Is something wrong?' Probably another of Kerry's Irish emotional storms, she conjectured resignedly, knowing she hadn't the stamina to cope with that at this moment. Her own emotions were twisted out of recognition by the events of the last couple of hours.

'Oh, Serena!' Kerry wailed, big tears spilling from her blue eyes as if the end of the world had come, as it frequently did with her.

'Shut up, Kerry,' the more practical Joanna quelled, getting to her feet and coming over to Serena. 'There's bad news, Serena. I'm sorry, darling, but it seems I have to be the purveyor of it. Your father had an accident on his boat today and he—didn't survive it.'

'But Daddy knows the sea better than anyone,' Serena protested numbly. 'There must be a mistake—he's probably holed up somewhere until a storm passes.'

'I'm sorry,' Joanna repeated gently, 'but there's no mistake. His boat was found floating aimlessly, and they think he may have gone for a swim and for some reason couldn't make it back to the boat.'

Serena shook her head negatively. 'No, you don't know my father. He's a strong swimmer, he'd have made it back.'

Another voice intruded into the fraught scene, a rough male voice that demanded belligerently, 'What about my fare, then? I'm losing good fare time, miss, while I sit out there waiting for you to come back and pay me!'

Joanna went and talked to him in a low voice and he said loudly, 'Oh, my Gawd, poor little lady! I'm sorry, miss, I wouldn't have dreamed of pressing you for the fare if I'd known. My condolences, I'm sure.'

Those words more than any Joanna or Kerry

could have uttered made real the fact of her father's death. Serena wailed in a high-pitched keening sound and wrapped her arms around the black dress that might have been an omen. With her father gone, with Benedict gone, she was completely alone in the world.

CHAPTER FOUR

'SET, and game. Not bad, Miss Howard,' David's muscular arm circled her waist as they walked off the court. 'All in all, I'd say we make a perfect team.'

In more ways than one, Serena thought affectionately, her smile matching his in brilliance. 'Against people twice our age, we're magnificent,' she teased.

'Well,' he conceded reluctantly, 'they are the champions of their retirement colony in Florida.'

'Which leaves us where?'

The Allens, Mamie and Doug, were fulsome in their praise of Windfair and its aura of Bermudian history. 'We'd sure like to take you up on your invitation to dinner here,' Doug said regretfully, 'but we promised to meet some friends from the States tonight.'

'Come on Saturday evening,' invited Serena, smiling. 'That's the night when we have a slide show commentated by the talented man who photographed Bermuda's salient spots and amalgamated his slides into an interesting melange of life on the islands.'

'We'd love that,' Mamie accepted enthusiastically, her eyes roving over the neat perfection of lawn and wealth of tropical flowers rioting uninhibitedly round it. 'I certainly hope he included Windfair in his spots to visit in Bermuda. To think that you're actually related to the

Captain Peregrine Howard who started all this! I can't wait to tell my bridge club back home.'

'Perhaps they wouldn't be so enamoured of him if they knew that he supported his mistress far more grandly than his wife,' Serena rejoined drily, nodding to the waitress who approached the table they occupied under the trees, indicating that tea would be welcome.

'You don't say!' Mamie exclaimed, awed yet curious as she took one of the wrought-iron chairs and pulled it in to the filigreed iron table.

'Oh yes, he considered his mistress a much more essential part of his life than his legitimate wife,' Serena informed her blandly. 'His wife, Matilda, provided the children who carried his name, but it was Julia Parker who retained his love until the day he died.'

'Isn't that romantic?' Mamie breathed reverently—although, Serena privately surmised, she would have been aghast if her Doug ventured into forbidden female territory.

'Not for his wife, I imagine.' David's dry tone changed to one of light teasing as he turned to smile at Serena. 'I hope your invitation to dinner still holds good for me. I have nothing pressing to do tonight.'

Serena returned his smile, comfortable with the easy intimacy between them now. They were friends as well as—well, if not lovers in the fullest sense, the basis was there for a long and happy life together.

'As if you have to wait for an invitation from your wife-to-be,' chuckled Mamie, her pale blue eyes openly admiring as they rested on David's clear-cut good looks. Women of all ages looked at David like that, Serena reflected, busying herself with the tea tray the maid had just placed on the table. It wasn't only that he was an attractive man physically, he had the kind of personality that drew people into the sunniness of his orbit ... a valuable asset in his business.

'She's very strict with the time she allows me,' David said with pseudo self-pity, although Serena thought she detected a glint of deeper meaning in the sherry brown eyes. 'Sometimes I don't see her for weeks at a time.'

'An exaggeration.' Serena calmly handed the tea-cups round, wrinkling her nose at him as she gave him his. 'I think one weekend went by when we didn't meet, and that was at the height of the yacht race season.'

Doug, a fresh-faced man despite his sixty-odd years and iron-grey hair, chuckled drily. 'I'm surprised you ever find any free time at all to be together. You seem to be on the go twenty-four hours a day, Dave, and I imagine the same goes for you, Serena.'

'Oh no, I'm not as dedicated as David,' she discounted. 'I leave most of the work to the people I've hired for just that purpose. That leaves me free to paint or do whatever takes my fancy.'

Mamie's interest quickened. 'David told us about your painting talent,' she leaned forward eagerly. 'Do you think we might see some of your work—maybe buy one of them?'

'Yes, of course you can see them, we'll stroll down to the cottage after tea if you like—but I assure you there's no obligation to buy. Money from that source isn't as important as it was when Windfair was getting on its feet as a commercial enterprise.'

Doug glanced round, his eyes encompassing the lovely old house with its louvred green shutters which, Bermuda fashion, opened from the bottom, the smooth emerald lawns and the relaxed guests taking tea, as they did, under the shade of pink poui trees. 'I admire your courage in tackling something like this on your own. You must have been very young, too.'

'I was,' Serena admitted, then slid a smile in David's direction, 'but I didn't do it all myself. It couldn't have been done without David's help.'

'I don't agree,' he contradicted quietly. 'I think you'd have done it even if it meant hanging wallpaper yourself or digging the beds for those flowers over there. You're a very determined lady.'

'It's like something you read in a book,' Mamie sighed happily, 'the two of you meeting and falling in love while you worked together on the changes to Windfair. So romantic.'

It hadn't been like that, Serena thought, remembering how determined she had been not to become involved in another relationship that could tear down her life again. But she had no intention of continuing the conversation on those lines, and she rose briskly, saying, 'Well, if you're ready we should go down and see the paintings now, or you're going to be late for your dinner date.'

The American couple showed delight in the cottage, Mamie exclaiming, 'It's so darling, and you can be completely self-contained here. I guess sometimes you need to be alone when the inspiration to paint strikes.'

Serena hid a smile of wry amusement. 'It isn't that so much, Mamie, as being forcibly consigned down here by my assistant when she needs my suite in the house for guests.'

'Is this your latest one?' asked David, arms crossed over his chest, legs solidly apart as he looked at the painting she had recently finished. 'It's good.'

'You say that about all my pictures,' she declined the compliment, smiling as she came to stand beside him, closely followed by Mamie.

'That's because they're all good,' he said with such sincere simplicity that Serena flashed him a look that was half pleasure, half tolerance for his prejudiced view. He would probably say the same if she threw paint haphazardly at the canvas and called it a 'mood' piece with only a title to pinpoint what she had meant by it.

'It's beautiful,' Mamie breathed at her shoulder. 'So typical of Bermuda. I'd love to buy it if it's still for sale. Doug, come and look at this.'

'You know I'm no judge of art, honey,' he protested, but he took eyeglasses from his shirt pocket to survey the painting more clearly. 'Why yes, this is really good, I've seen a dozen lanes in Bermuda that look just like it. How much are you asking for it, Serena?'

She hated the commercial aspect of her work. Each painting was like a child she only unwillingly parted from, and her agent in Hamilton always realised far better prices than she was inclined to ask privately.

'Well, I . . .'

'It would go for four hundred dollars in Hamilton,' David smoothly inserted, 'but I'm sure we can persuade Serena to part with it for, say, three hundred and fifty?'

Serena's murmured protest was overruled by
Mamie's instant assault on Doug's more canny
nature. 'I like it so much better than that one we
bought for a thousand dollars in New York last
year, honey. When I tell the girls that this was
painted by a descendant of the Peregrine Howard
who started the estate of Windfair, they'll be pea-
green with envy!'

Her paintings had been bought for many
reasons over the last few years, Serena thought,
but never one as blatantly expressed as this, at
least not to her knowledge. But why should she
carp at Mamie's twisted reasoning when she
herself had made full capital of her relationship to
the notorious Peregrine? Visitors to Windfair
revelled in the lore associated with his name.

'Don't worry,' David murmured as they filed
out of the cottage, 'they won't have to scrimp and
save from their pension to buy it, they're not
lacking a dollar or two.'

'That isn't the point,' she argued in an
undertone, turning to lock the cottage door
although her hiding place for the key was a pot of
full-headed geraniums on the porch, the first place
a potential burglar would have looked. 'I hate the
thought that they'll think they've been had once
they get back to their home surroundings.'

'Why do you underrate yourself so much?' he
frowned impatiently as they followed the other
couple who had gone ahead. 'In some ways you're
so confident, Serena, and in others ...' He
stopped, his mouth clamping down on the words
he might have spoken.

Words he never did speak, Serena thought as
they followed a leisurely pace back to the house,

the conversation of the others needing no response from her apart from a smile now and then. Words that might have changed the status quo between them, and neither of them wanted that. She loved David with all the affection that was in her ... if true passion was missing from their relationship now, their marriage would break down the last of her inhibitions against giving herself totally in body as well as mind. Only a man with David's understanding and restraint would have waited this long for a consummation that would have raised no brows in an engaged couple. In any couple these days, it seemed.

'What do you think, Serena?'

She looked up at the sound of David's voice and saw three curious pairs of eyes scanning her own, which felt dazed. 'I'm sorry, I—I was thinking of something else.'

'No prize for the one who guesses the subject of your thoughts,' Doug Allen said with heavy humour, lifting his thick grey brows.

Mamie chimed in archly, 'I don't see why you two plan on waiting all that time to get married— why not do it while we're here, and we can attend the wedding.'

Something more to retail to her bridge friends, Serena thought uncharitably. She liked the older couple, and that they still seemed to like each other was a good omen for the possibility of a long, happy relationship. 'I'm afraid we had to lay our plans very carefully so that we can both be away together,' she explained quickly.

Doug chuckled. 'It just struck me—where does a couple go for a honeymoon when they live in a lovers' paradise like Bermuda?'

'That's privileged information,' said David firmly. 'Not even Serena knows yet.' He turned to her. 'Well, what *do* you think about playing a return match at Moongate on Saturday? Then you can reverse today's process and have dinner with us.'

'I'd love the return match, but I'll have to take a raincheck on the dinner. We've some new arrivals coming on Saturday, and you know I like to be around for their first evening.'

'Sunday, then?'

'Perhaps.' Moments later they parted at the parking lot outside the house. David had decided to drive the Allens back to Moongate and change for dinner there.

As was usual at mid-week, the dining room was less congested than at weekends, and Serena felt no qualms at choosing her favourite table for her dinner with David. In a corner, flanked by floor-length windows, potted feathery palms gave it an air of seclusion. The pristine white of the starched tablecloth took on a pink hue from the red glass hurricane lamp with its steadily burning candle, and red hibiscus blossoms floating in a low crystal dish added to that effect.

Low as the candlelight was, the large sliding doors leading to the terrace were closed against insects attracted to the flickering glow from every table, but the temperature in the dining room was temperate enough for low-necked and sleeveless dresses to be worn in comfort, while the men dressed in regulation jacket and tie felt the rule was no imposition.

'Just looking at you,' Serena told David softly

across the table, 'makes me so glad I made the rule about jackets and ties. It makes a woman feel,' she shrugged, 'oh, I don't know, special somehow if the man with her makes an effort.'

'And the same in reverse.' His eyes, a darker brown in the dimmed light, dropped to the expanse of honey-toned flesh visible above the soft gathering of straw-coloured silk across her breasts, her arms and shoulders bare except for a halter of the same material snaking up round her slender neck. 'Have I seen that dress before?'

'Men!' Serena raised her eyes towards the ceiling where purely decorative fans circulated slowly. 'You must have seen it a dozen times or more.'

'Then there's something different about your hair—your make-up?' he hazarded when she shook her head.

'My hair is the same as it always is.' It was indeed sleeked back into a French twist she was adept at achieving now. Relief from severity was provided by a few tendrils pulled out and the dexterous use of a curling iron. 'The trouble with you is that you're surrounded by too many nymphets in bikinis and divorcees laying their all before you to notice what Miss Howard of Windfair is wearing at any particular time,' she teased, sipping vermouth as they waited for the first course to arrive.

David's groan was too deep-throated to be insincere. 'If I see one more nubile female accidentally-on-purpose dropping one strap of her bikini top to expose her as yet uninteresting bosom to me, I swear I'll do what her father should have done years ago with great regularity!'

Serena laughed, only too well aware of the

adolescents who fell heavily for his good looks, his charm that extended to everyone in his orbit, weaving sexual fantasies around him in the same way as they would for a current pop star. 'Don't be too hard on them, darling. Girls go through strange phases on the way to growing up, especially where older men are concerned.' A sudden gust of remembrance brought a tightness to her throat. Dear God, yes ... how attractive those older men could be to a girl impatient to sample all of life's wares! Men old enough to know better than to tamper with untried emotions ...

'What's wrong, Serena?' David spoke quietly, his eyes intent as he stretched a hand across the table to grasp hers. 'Something's been bothering you all day—care to tell me what it is?'

She shrugged lightly and forced a smile, twisting her hand round until it lay under his. 'Just silly ghosts walking over my grave for no reason.'

His gaze dropped to where his fingers rubbed gently against her skin. 'Ghosts don't usually walk unless there's a damn good reason, especially where you're concerned. Would I be right if I guessed that your spectres have something to do with what happened in London years ago?'

Serena gasped and gave him a stricken look. He understood her well ... too well on this occasion. He knew about Benedict, if not by name then by what had happened between them; she would not have agreed to marry him otherwise, in spite of his assurances that what had happened in either of their lives had no bearing on their future together. The subject had never been raised again in the six months of their engagement, until now.

'It's just that—someone of the same name

telephoned from London this morning to make a booking,' she told him honestly in a low voice. 'It's not the same man—this one has a daughter, and Be—he didn't. I suppose it just—stirred things up in my mind again, things I haven't wanted to remember for years now.'

David's fingers tightened on her hand, not hurtfully but making her aware of the pressure. 'Are you sure of that, Serena?' he asked quietly.

She frowned, puzzled. 'Sure of what? If you mean am I sure I've put all that behind me, then the answer is yes. You know that—if it still meant anything to me I wouldn't have agreed to marry you.'

'I know,' he smiled somewhat wryly, 'but stuffing it to the back of your mind doesn't necessarily mean that you don't still feel something for this man. Don't they say a woman never gets over her first love?'

Her heart had begun a rapid, painful rhythm, but from anger, not the fear that he might be right. She withdrew her hand and said frostily, 'If you think that's true in my case, perhaps we'd better re-think our relationship. Marriage without trust is no marriage at all.' Her small white teeth bit down on the fullness of her lower lip, and she felt a ridiculous prickling of tears behind her eyes. What had got into David tonight? It was as if a beloved pet she'd had for years had suddenly turned round to bite her. He made no effort to recapture her hand, but stared thoughtfully at her.

'I agree,' he said slowly. 'That's why I decided to speak to you about it tonight. It struck me today—belatedly, I admit—when the Allens asked why we don't get married right away, that there was no reason in the world why we shouldn't do just that.'

Serena blinked. 'But we've made all the arrangements for June,' she began.

'No, Serena, *you* made the arrangements for June, I just went along with that date because—well, I suppose I thought you wanted time to be really sure. Now I wonder if you'll ever be sure. I love you, Serena,' he continued huskily, 'and if you said to me tonight, "Let's get married tomorrow" I'd move heaven and earth to get the licence in time. What would your reaction be if I said to you, "Let's get married tomorrow"?'

Serena's fingers found the fork on her left and she unconsciously began to make precise grooves in the stiff tablecloth. 'That's not a fair question,' she said in a low voice he had to strain to catch. 'I couldn't just up and leave Windfair at a moment's notice, we're packed to the roof with bookings . . .'

' "I leave most of the work to the people I've hired for just that purpose",' he quoted softly her own words to the Allens that afternoon.

'That's unfair!' she retorted hotly, repeating her previous accusation. 'Taking a few hours off during the slack time of the day to paint is a long way from disappearing altogether for weeks on end!'

David sat back when Joseph arrived with their crab cocktails, and Serena felt a sharp sense of relief for the breathing space. She had never known David like this, doggedly persistent in face of her obvious distress. It made her feel insecure, as if a rock she had trusted her weight to had suddenly begun to shift. A flush swept up to her cheeks when she saw Joseph's puckered brow, his anxious glance going from one strained face to the other. Every member of the staff adored David, and approved her choice of husband to share the running of Windfair. There had never been the ghost of an argument between them before, and Serena well understood how the older black man felt. He would no doubt share his insecurity with Matty, at least, and Serena would be subjected to one of the old housekeeper's lectures on her headstrong foolishness. But that wasn't what truly concerned her as she laid aside the fork she had been using to push the sauce-covered crab sections from one spot to the other in its dish. David, she noted, wasn't making much more headway with his. A hard lump in her throat made it hard to speak past it, and her words came out like strangled gasps.

'I can't make it tomorrow, but—do you think you can get the licence for next week?'

His head jerked back and his eyes met hers with almost audible impact. 'What?'

'If that's what it takes to prove that I love you and not some spectre from the past, then I want us to be married as soon as possible.' The shock reflected in his face strangely lent confidence to her own flagging courage. 'Or were you just talking through your hat?'

His hands reached across the table to pin hers to the starched coolness of the cloth. 'I don't possess a hat,' he said with more solemnity than the words merited, 'but if I did, I wouldn't use it to talk through. God, Serena, I—I don't know what to say. I suppose I was—testing you when I said that about getting married tomorrow.' His eyes seemed

a darker brown than ever as they roved
incredulously over her face. 'You really mean it?'

She nodded, knowing that he was no more
interested in the *filet de boeuf au Madère* to follow
the crab than she herself was. She wanted badly to
feel the solid security of his arms around her, to
yield her mouth to the seeking warmth of his.
Even, for the first time, to submit to his total
possession. Fright at the thought of losing him had
finally driven out the memory of Benedict
Ramsey. It was David she loved, wanted to spend
the rest of her life with. A weight seemed to be
lifted from her heart, and she smiled with the
tenderness born of love as David's incredulity
changed to buoyant acceptance.

'Let's get out of here,' he demanded thickly, 'we
can't discuss our future with so many curious eyes
watching us.'

Serena smiled with programmed grace to the
patrons enjoying Windfair's atmosphere and food
as she made her way through the dining room,
pausing to say to a puzzled Joseph, 'We're not
very hungry after all, but we'd like coffee in the
office whenever you have time.'

Clive, the student from the hotel training college
who replaced Pat on evenings and at weekends,
smiled shyly when they passed the reception desk
on their way to the office beyond.

'Everything all right?' Serena murmured.

'Just fine, Miss Howard.'

The office seemed a haven of quiet after the
clatter of dishes, the sudden spurts of loud
laughter in the dining room. It was like another
world, a world of quiet elegance which Charles
Howard had no doubt appreciated even without

the knowledge that strangers inhabited his family home. Serena had long since faced the fact that he would probably have resented the strangers who gazed enraptured at relics denoting the past of Windfair, who slept in rooms redolent with Windfair's history, who bathed in modern bathrooms unknown in his day.

She went willingly into the arms David held out to her, lifting her lips to the hard possession of his. Her hands spread on the muscled tautness of his chest and felt the harsh beat of his heart under her palms, a beat that made her own pulses dance to its rhythm. Her slender body lifted and moulded itself to the forceful impact of his, feeling the sinewy male muscles that tautened against the soft surge of her thighs.

Desire licked like searing flames from nerve end to nerve end as Serena clung to the moist warmth of David's shirt front, her senses spiralling into a dizzy orbit of stark need she knew exultantly that he would fill beyond her wildest imaginings. Her knees would have buckled beneath her but for the banded hardness of his arm to support her.

Joseph's soft knocking at the door came as a wrenching reminder of the world inexorably turning on its axis outside its thick oak panels, and Serena reluctantly pulled away from the lips that went immediately to the vulnerable softness under her ear, then traced a searing path to the firm rise of flesh straining against the folded silk confining her breasts.

'David . . .' Her breath sighed in her throat, the precious knowledge that she could, at last, give herself to David in body as well as mind shivering through her like a cleansing wind. Yet still she

tensed when Joseph came in at her tremulous
summons, a pleased smile creasing the barely
noticeable lines around his eyes and mouth. All
was well again with his world; Miss Serena and the
man she was to marry had made up their quarrel.

With the sixth sense David possessed in
abundance, he picked up on her reluctance to
share the brought-forward date of their marriage.
Time enough for that when the new arrangements
were firmed and irrevocable.

No definite date had been arranged when Serena
drove herself to Moongate the following Saturday,
and she was torn between a treacherous relief and
a sense of letdown. Relief because she had known
the morning after the dinner with David that she
had acted with unusual impetuosity in saying she
would marry him within a week. She had reacted
to the odd mood he himself had been in that night
and she couldn't bear to see him hurt. That's how
it was when you cared for someone, she'd told
herself endlessly, warding off the cold panic that
began to fill her within hours. Instead of months
to prepare for the serious business of marriage,
there were frighteningly few hours left to her now.

Her own vacillation irritated her. Another part
of her had known peace of a sort, that a decision
had been made and there was no turning back
from it. She loved David, and she would be a good
wife to him, the kind of wife he deserved. There
wasn't the desperate clutching of the passionate
love she'd felt for Benedict all those years ago; she
doubted now if what she had felt had been more
than a child's greedy need to experience everything
in life too eagerly, too soon.

She drove into the hotel's courtyard parking area and commandeered one of the spaces marked 'Reserved', her thoughts growing less intense as she walked towards the low, Tudor-style hotel which had become as familiar to her as Windfair over the past few months.

The inn had changed with the years, more especially since David had taken over its management; the spirit of the buccaneers still lingered in the scuffed and battered sea-chests scattered here and there, in the paint-chipped mermaid in the low-ceilinged lounge-hall who had once graced the prow of the *Dorset Belle* and who had survived the shipwreck which had taken master and men and good British oak to their watery grave in the ocean's rocky bottom off Bermuda.

But those old renegades would never recognise the modern amenities David had introduced . . . a private bathroom for each bedroom, comfortably sprung mattresses in place of straw pallets, central air cooling the inn to a comfortable temperature. There was even a separate room where the younger element could disco until the early hours. It amused Serena to reflect sometimes on what the reactions would be of the hardbitten buccaneers who roared lustily about a maid in Amsterdam who was mistress of her trade to the unstructured music of the late twentieth century.

David was chatting casually with a couple in their forties who were seated on one of the blue and white upholstered rattan sofas in the comfortable lounge area. As always, he looked completely unhurried and as if he wanted to be there with them more than anything in the world. But, knowing him well, she caught the quick glint of relief in his eyes when she walked over to them. Standing, he stretched out a hand to take hers and dropped a kiss on her forehead before turning to the couple looking curiously up at them and introducing her as his fiancée.

While the male half of the pair stood to shake Serena's hand, the woman seemed too surprised to move from the sofa. 'You amaze me, Mr Storey, I'd have thought some lucky girl would have snatched you away long ago.' Then her plump face took on a stricken look. 'Oh, I'm sorry, Miss Howard, that wasn't very tactful of me, was it?'

'Don't worry,' Serena smiled, 'I'm used to it—and yes, I do consider myself lucky.' David's hand tightened on hers as she extended the smile to him. Murmuring that he had promised her lunch, he pulled her away, but only as far as the reception desk inside the main doors.

'Look, Serena, do you mind going ahead? With this yacht race business and people pouring in for it, we're all in a flap.'

'Not you, David,' she mocked lightly. 'Everyone else, perhaps, but never you.'

'You don't know what chaos there is behind this calm exterior of mine.' The girl on duty behind the desk, a pretty, round-faced Bermudian, shyly interrupted them, giving Serena an apologetic smile.

'Mr Storey, can you see the couple in 102 who arrived this morning? They say they prefer a quieter room overlooking the garden, but everything I have there is taken. The man insists on talking to you about it.'

'All right, Terri, I'll——' Suddenly remembering that the hand he still held was Serena's, a rare frown creased his brow. 'I'm really sorry about this, darling, but I'll join you in the Mariner Room as soon as I can. I've reserved a table for us, they're expecting you, and maybe you'll order for me too?'

Hardly waiting for her nod of agreement, he turned back to the desk and, smiling wryly to herself, Serena made her way to the dining room situated overlooking the Harbour. It was a familiar scene to her, putting guests before personal concerns, but David was like a mother hen determined to oversee every one of her chicks herself. No delegation, or very little. But that was David.

The dining room staff greeted her with friendly smiles, and she was ushered to the table David had reserved by one of the windows immediately overlooking the water.

'Mr Storey won't be along for a little while,' she told the waiter who settled her into a view chair, 'he's been held up.'

'When is he not, Miss Howard?' he posed wryly. 'Would you like to have a drink while you wait?'

'Yes, I suppose I could do that, although he's asked me to order for him. I'll have lager and lime, please, Paul, and I'll look at the menu while I drink that.'

There was a pleasant atmosphere in the timbered, low-ceilinged dining room, which was much less formal than Windfair's. Most of the lunchers had finished eating and were drifting off to other pursuits. Casual seagoing clothes seemed the order of the day for the men, and some of their wives or girl-friends too; obviously they were here for the yacht races taking place during the next week. A few male eyes glanced with interest in Serena's direction, but evidently decided that in her pale lemon shirtwaist dress with its white high-necked collar and demure half sleeves she was too elegant to share their boating interest.

David, looking unrushed but moving rapidly nonetheless, joined her moments after she had ordered from the menu. 'I hope you're in the mood for cucumber salad to start with and broiled sole to follow,' she queried as he took the chair opposite and sighed gustily.

'Sounds perfect, although I think I'll alter the sequence of things and start with a stiff drink instead.' Seeming to sense that he was needed, Paul appeared at his side. 'Double Scotch and water, please, Paul.'

'Goodness, you must have had a strained morning,' said Serena lightly.

'It's been a strained week all round, and worse to come.' He gave her a tired smile and loosened the tie at his neck; come hell or high water, David set the standard of neat dressing in his hotel staff. 'Perhaps I should take your advice and hire people who are capable of taking over now and then.'

'You already have the people,' she pointed out, draining the last of her lager and setting the glass aside, 'it's just that you can't seem to let go the reins and let them function at full capacity.'

Paul set his drink before him and he took a deep draught of it before looking ruefully at her. 'You know me too well,' he said softly. 'or do I mean well enough to make me the best possible wife.' It wasn't a question as such, more a simple statement of contented fact. An unexpected flutter from inside caught Serena unaware, but before she had

time to analyse the feeling David was speaking
again, apology in his voice.

'And while we're on that subject, I have to
report that there's very little to report. The yacht
races evidently affect more than beleaguered
hoteliers. It's difficult to get people interested in a
hastily arranged wedding, especially when they all
know us and that June has been the date to look
forward to. I was even looked at with a fair
amount of loathing when their little minds worked
out the only feasible reason why I should want to
marry you in a hurry.'

'Oh, David, I'm sorry.' How embarrassing it
must have been for him to have clerks in
government offices stare at him in morbid
fascination as the despoiler of one of Bermuda's
most aristocratic families.

'No problem,' he shrugged, 'it's just that—well,
bringing forward the date might be a tremendously
romantic gesture, but quite honestly, Serena, it
poses a lot more problems than it solves.'

She stared at him, not certain if the sudden
lurching leap of her heart signified disappointment
or—relief. 'Y-you mean,' she stammered, 'we
should stick to the original arrangement?'

'Something like that,' he nodded, his hand
reaching for hers across the table. 'Perhaps not as
long as June, but—well, it's damn hard to alter the
arrangements I've made for the honeymoon,
especially since the weather won't be ideal at the
moment. Will you mind very much if we set a new
date for, say, March or April?'

Serena shook her head, knowing it was what he
wanted her to do but uncertain of her own
feelings. 'Of course not, if that's what we must do,'

she said practically, and felt his fingers tighten on hers.

'That's one of the things I like about you, Serena,' he said with the ghost of a smile, 'you take everything in your stride, even the prospect of being married within a week instead of the six months or more you'd expected. I did rush you on that, didn't I?'

Her head moved in a gesture of denial. 'It—was what I wanted too, David.'

'Was it? Or was it just that I was in such a bloody mood the other night that you took pity on me?' His mouth twisted into a wry curve. 'I'm afraid things here had been getting to me, and I took it out on you. I shouldn't have, but I did. Forgive me?'

'There's nothing to forgive.' With that shaky statement the conversation ended, with no time for it to be resurrected before the return tennis match with the Allens. Serena had brought her tennis clothes in an overnight bag, and she changed in David's private apartment on the ground floor of the hotel. It was as well, she reflected on Mamie's enthusiastic greeting, that the advanced date of the wedding hadn't been made public. As it was, no explanations were necessary.

It was a seemingly hard-fought game, although Serena suspected that David flubbed a few points to give the Allens a supremacy that won the game. Her heart twisted in bittersweet recognition of his goodness ... the older couple could go back to boast about their prowess over a younger, very fit couple in Bermuda.

They took tea on the rear terrace of the inn, and Serena decided to wear her tennis clothes home so that she could shower and change there for the dinner party that evening. She took her leave admist a chorus of 'See you at seven,' and 'See you later,' David coming to the car with her and necessarily restricted to a peck on the cheek by the hotel guests who thronged the courtyard.

'At seven?' he murmured, his eyes a soft brown reflecting the release physical exertion had given him.

She nodded, and stowed the bag containing her dress in the passenger seat beside her. A glow of warmth coloured her vision a rosy pink as she directed her small car towards Windfair. Everything seemed to have settled back into place in the few hours she had spent at Moongate. Knowing that there was no immediate hurry to assemble a honeymoon wardrobe at such short notice lifted an enormous burden from her shoulders. There was time—oodles of time—to prepare for a March or April wedding. Darling David ... he worked too hard, but that was something she could busy herself with in the months, the years to come.

Clive gave her a shy smile when she paused at the desk in the hall, and she wished the hotel student relaxed like that more often, it made him seem so much more human, so attractive. His life seemed to be haunted by the dread that Serena would report unfavourably on him to the Hotel School, and nothing could have been further from her mind.

'Did the new arrivals check in?' she asked, her eyes going automatically to the register open before him on the desk. Unlike Pat, he seemed to survive remarkably well without oceans of notes littering the area beside the telephone.

'Yes, Miss Howard. The Ellises are very happy with their room, and the——' he leaned over the register to refresh his memory, 'the Ramseys are settled into their suite. The poor little girl,' he inserted a rare private opinion, 'seems so sad. She clings to her father as if he's the only one she can trust.'

'That's understandable,' Serena returned absently. 'I believe her mother died last week.'

'Yes.'

'Oh, Clive,' she turned back from her progress across the hall to the stairs, 'would you make sure that there's a table reserved for me and three guests tonight? I mentioned it to Joseph, but he might get carried away with the Saturday night crowd.'

'Of course, Miss Howard.' Clive's smile reached confidently to his eyes this time, and Serena's mouth quirked in response as she headed for the stairs, her long legs tanned to Bermuda gold under the short white of her tennis skirt. She would have time for a relaxing soak in the tub and a leisurely dressing before David and the Allens arrived.

She glanced up to the staircase as a shadowy movement impinged on her consciousness, the remnants of her smile still curving her mouth as she looked at the man descending the stairs, a small girl scarcely visible behind the smoothly tailored trouser leg.

'Hello, Serena,' Benedict said gently.

CHAPTER FIVE

SOUND roared like an angry sea in her ears, and her legs felt as if they would be borne from under her by the sheer force of the storm that assaulted her senses. She swayed, wanting the oblivion of a faint into unconsciousness; her hand groped for and found the solidity of wood balustrade under her clutching fingers. Her eyes took in details she would only remember later, much later.

His face still held the rugged good-looking features she remembered, but there the resemblance ended. It was as if a sculptor's hand had wielded a cruel knife to etch deep lines around his eyes and mouth—particularly his mouth. Not lines ... gouges that bit deep into the once-malleable flesh and left traces like scars from nose to mouth.

'Benedict.' The word floated almost inaudibly between them, and he said nothing as her eyes shifted to the child clinging desperately to the fine worsted encasing his tensely muscled leg. A tangle of dark hair inexpertly confined with incongruously gaudy glass beads stretched on dark brown elastic; a dress that fell in limp salmon folds about a painfully thin figure; eyes that stared distrustfully out to an unfriendly world ... eyes that bore the same light grey opaqueness that marked her as Benedict's daughter.

From somewhere came a tautly controlled, 'Your daughter can eat right now in the dining room, Mr Ramsey. We prefer that children eat

separately from parents. If you'll excuse me.' She
stepped up the stairs to a point above them and
heard a small, bewildered voice whispering, 'Why
is the lady so angry, Daddy?'

The lady is angry, Serena responded silently as
she went to her suite on the first floor, because
Daddy made a fool of her years ago, when you
were—oh God, two years old! How was it possible
that Benedict could conceal a child of his loins
while exercising those loins on a naïve idiot who
believed he loved her as she loved him?

A scalding hot shower after stripping off her
tennis clothes did little to soothe the deep-seated
anger spreading rampantly to every point of her
being. How dared Benedict turn up here as if his
wife's death freed him finally from the ties that
bound him! Did he really expect that she would
fall into his arms, grateful that now she could be
his completely?

Damn him, damn him, and damn him again!
She didn't love him, she hated him with a passion
whose roots reached into her very soul. All the
agonised dreams of revenge surfaced again, with
more virulence than they had ever possessed. He,
and his child, had no place at Windfair ... she
would make that very clear at the first opportunity.

Her calm was icy when she left her suite and
descended to the hall where, moments later, David
and the Allens would be joining her. Clive looked
up questioningly as she approached.

'I think Mr Ramsey and his daughter would be
happier in a hotel catering to children,' she said
coolly. 'Phone round, Clive, and see what
accommodation you can find for them, will you?'

'Yes, Miss Howard.'

'I'll be in the dining room with my guests when you've made arrangements,' she added, turning to the door with perfect timing as David ushered the Allens into the lofty hall.

'Welcome to Windfair,' she greeted, gracious in a pale green dress that emphasised the shadowed area between her breasts while conveying the ladylike unconcern for physical charms instilled in her by a vigilant Matty. 'We have time to see the most important historical aspects of the house before we go into dinner. This hall, for instance, was once the Great Room Sir Peregrine Howard planned in great detail. It was here that he entertained his old shipmates as well as the notables of the Colony . . .'

Mamie and Doug Allen were among the easiest of visitors to Windfair, their awed interest undiscriminating as they followed her round the main hall and gaped at the portraits hanging there. David stood back, appreciating as Serena did the historical significance of Windfair without now being unduly impressed with it.

Serena stopped before the portrait of a thick-bearded man whose green eyes looked boldly out from the canvas as if impatient to return to the sea his eyes reflected. 'This is Peregrine Howard,' she announced solemnly, 'the man who built Windfair from his profits as a privateer.'

'Oh my,' Mamie breathed, 'it's certainly obvious that you're descended from him—look at those eyes!'

'And this is his wife, Matilda,' Serena went on smoothly, seeing a shadowy movement from the corner of her eye, sensing that it was Benedict who paused on the stairs to listen. She kept her eyes trained on the portrait of Matilda, her chastely parted brown hair and rather plain face in contrast to the woman who stood, hands on hips, boldly looking out on the world in the next portrait.

'And this is Julia, Peregrine's illicit love,' she explained in a tight voice, which nevertheless carried to the man hesitating halfway down the staircase. 'She was very beautiful, the belle of every sea captain coming to haven in Bermuda. But it was Peregrine Howard who caught her fancy, and she loved him faithfully until the day she died of typhoid at the age of thirty-three. His wife, no doubt, felt relieved to be rid of the woman who had stolen her husband from her. She and Peregrine lived out their days in the peaceful security of the marriage bond.'

She had often wondered just how peaceful those days had been for Peregrine; wasn't it natural that his wife, the mother of his children, should resent to the last the woman who had usurped her husband and turned his eyes from hearth and home to the more exotic delights Julia Parker offered? She had often felt an affinity for the ill-fated Julia who gave so much for so little return. She had loved Peregrine, and braved the censure of their world to prove it. Still, Matilda deserved at least respect for her adherence to the vows that had bound her and Peregrine together. Pain must have been a close adjunct to the joy their union brought.

'I think I'd have told him to make his choice between her and me,' Mamie volunteered thoughtfully, her gaze divided between the voluptuous attractions of Julie Parker with her lustrous, slightly waving dark hair, and the trusting honesty looking steadfastly out from Matilda's portrait. 'She looks—defenceless somehow, as if Peregrine was all she had, and if he left her for this other woman she'd take it, but she'd rather be dead.'

An odd pain worked its way under Serena's heart. Benedict's wife *was* dead, but she'd need a far greater imagination than she possessed to believe that Caroline Ramsey would take her life because of another woman in her husband's life. She must have been too sure that Benedict would always return to her, if only to secure the goal his ambition had set.

'Over here was the parlour, used by Peregrine and his family for relaxing privately,' she stepped graciously into the lead as she crossed the hall, schooling herself to meet Benedict's eyes with a blank stare. Where was the child? she wondered; only a short time ago she had been clinging with a sort of desperation to Benedict's trousers, so she could hardly believe she had agreed to stay alone in their suite while he came down to dinner. Forcing her thoughts back to the task she was engaged in, she managed a light laugh as the group entered the room which faced out to the front; a small room in comparison with others in the living area, but still large in today's world of compact architecture. 'I'm not sure how relaxing it was in here, what with horsehair sofas and upright chairs. As you can see, it's much more comfortably furnished now and our guests find it pleasantly quiet for reading or writing or just—relaxing!'

Serena had gone to the opposite extreme with the furnishings, large, deep-cushioned sofas and chairs in restful green and beige, paler green carpeting adding to the tranquil atmosphere.

'My, you did all this yourself?' asked Mamie in wonder as she glanced round. 'You could have had a career as an interior designer!'

David slid an arm round her waist as they left the room, hugging her to his side as he dropped a kiss near her temple, pride in his brown eyes as he looked down into hers. 'That's only one of her many talents.'

'You wouldn't be just a little prejudiced?' she teased back, moving away from his hold to lead the way into the dining room.

'Certainly I am, and I intend to stay that way.'

Serena had expected that Benedict would have made his way into the dining room by now, and she stopped short when he turned from the portrait of Peregrine to stare levelly at her, a strange, haunted look in his almost opaque grey eyes. Colour rushed into her face, then ebbed again as quickly, leaving her pale. He must have seen David's arm around her, the kiss, and heard the possessive note in his voice. So what, the harsh thought came as she moved forward once more. Unlike him years before, David was free to bestow his affections wherever he wished. There was no wife in his background to make that bestowal a furtive thing.

Still, she was distracted as she settled into her chair at her favourite table. The dining room was crowded and noisy as was usual on Saturday evenings, but she knew immediately when Benedict took his place at a table for two near the entrance doors. Where *was* that child of his? The thought nagged at her until she was forced to admit that Benedict's daughter, with her pinched, miserable-looking face, had raised a protective instinct

Serena hadn't known she possessed. Her father obviously had no idea of how to care for her, that much was obvious from her waif-like appearance. Had he locked her into the suite while he came down looking fit for a gala evening in black dinner jacket and snowy white shirt?

'Serena?' She jerked back to present reality when David spoke her name sharply, evidently not for the first time.

'I'm sorry, I—I was a million miles away,' she apologised, realising belatedly that her guests at the table might look on that as an affront to their importance.

David evidently looked on her distraction that way, because his voice had an astringent quality she had never heard from him before when he said tersely, 'Mamie is interested in what this room was used for in Peregrine's day.'

'Oh . . . well, this was originally a ballroom where Peregrine could entertain the élite of Bermuda society,' she launched into a bright description of the society of that day. The words came out like a well-remembered rote, which they were. For the first time in her memory the recital became a bore to her . . . Peregrine Howard had reaped more of life's rewards than he was entitled to, she realised suddenly. A wife who adored him to the end, despite his perfidy, and a mistress who wound steely bands of enchantment round him. In those days, a peccadillo or two on the side were tolerated, if not expected. Benedict would have been much more at home in that age than his own, she decided sourly, glancing again at the table near the doors with a venom Benedict must have caught, because he was staring right across the room at her.

She seemed perfectly in control as the conversation flowed between her and her guests, but underneath a powerful cauldron bubbled and threatened to explode. How dared he come here, she reiterated the question while smiling brilliantly at a remark of Doug's, and plunge her life into chaos again? His dead wife, strangely, had no bearing on it at all, except that she had Serena's heartfelt condolences at having been married to Benedict. She wasn't foolish enough to imagine that she had been the only woman he had found beddable, if not weddable. An endless string of attractive, nubile girls paraded before her inner vision . . . God, how she hated him!

Clive came up to her as she, David and the Allens left the dining room. 'I'm sorry, Miss Howard,' he said abjectly, 'but I've tried everywhere, and there's no room anywhere for Mr Ramsey and his daughter. The yacht races, you see . . .'

The yacht races. Yes, of course, she had forgotten the influx of visitors for the international events being staged in Bermuda this coming week.

'What's wrong, darling?' David came back to ask.

'Nothing,' she rejoined swiftly. Telling him that she had two more guests than she was willing to accommodate would have entailed too much explanation. And David wasn't a fool. He would know immediately that Benedict wasn't in the usual run of visitors to Windfair. That he meant something deeper to her . . . She linked her arm with his and said in a loud voice Benedict would have no trouble hearing, 'A man and his daughter just arrived today, and I felt they might be more comfortable in a place more orientated to children. Windfair isn't exactly geared to children . . .'

She felt genuinely sad when the Allens made their farewells. 'Let us know when the wedding's to be, and we'll come back to Bermuda for it,' Doug promised huskily as he kissed her cheek. 'Mamie would never forgive me if she didn't get to attend the wedding of the year.'

Serena murmured pleasantries, and was unforgivably glad when David gave her a perfunctory kiss on the cheek before striding to the car park to perform his duty of driving them back to his hotel. She loved him—had she ever doubted it? Their lives were meshed both in business and in a personal sense. They were right for each other, every facet of their relationship pointed to that fact.

Normally she would have stayed in sight of the visitors and guests who filled Windfair's dining room to capacity on Saturday night, but on this occasion she escaped to the privacy of her suite on the first floor, though peace avoided her even there.

A rhythmic keening floated through the stout door panels of the suite next to her own, and Serena listened unashamedly to the lullabies that had soothed her to sleep long after she had reached the age Benedict's daughter now was. So it was Matty who had made it possible for Benedict to leave his daughter and dine alone! Matty with her soft heart and friendly bosom, a child's panacea in a bewildering adult world.

In her own bedroom, she stripped off the clothes she had worn that evening and went naked to the shower, welcoming its soothing cleanse of memory-filled pores. The rounded tilt of her breasts dripped moisture from their rosy tips to the flat stomach and slenderly muscled thighs below them and ran in abstract channels down the length of her legs to merge with the soapy surge towards the central drain. The deluge left her body stringently clean, but Serena still felt soiled as she reached for the thirsty thickness of the towel neatly arranged on the rail and buffed the honey-gold of her body skin with it.

The oyster silk full-length robe hanging behind the bathroom door stuck momentarily to her moist skin, then clung like a limpet to the soft swell of breast and hip as she stepped into the adjoining bedroom. Her hand stilled in the act of flipping out the thick tangle of her hair from the robe's collar when a figure rose from the cosy seating arrangement flanking her bedroom window.

'How the hell did you get in here?' she asked hoarsely, and saw Benedict shrug under the cover of his black dinner jacket.

'The door was unlocked and you didn't hear my knock,' he explained in a voice that sent twinges of remembrance rocketing through her.

'I've never felt it necessary to lock my door—until now.' She felt at a disadvantage, her hair dripping moisture to her collar, her face shinily free of make-up, deserted by her usual poise. How ironic! On the few occasions when she had allowed herself to imagine this unlikely confrontation with Benedict, she had been cool, calm, incisive and dressed to match. 'However, you may be sure that when you walk through that door in ten seconds from now, I shall make a point of barring it against your re-entry. Get out, Benedict—now!'

A cold pinning with his grey eyes and a hard jut of his square jaw told her he had no intention of obeying the order. 'I'll go when you've heard what I came to say, and not before. Now, are you going to be civilised and sit down, or——'

'Civilised!' she choked on the word. 'Do you call breaking into my bedroom and threatening me civilised?'

'I didn't break into your room, the door was open,' he repeated almost wearily. 'I came to you here because it seems this is the only place where we can talk in peace.'

'What unmitigated gall you have!' Serena was beginning to achieve the coolness she prided herself on, the control that reminded her not to demonstrate how shattered she had been to see him again. 'What makes you think we have any point in common to discuss? I talk with my friends, Benedict,' she scathed, 'and I talk with my guests, but there's no room in my life for renewing old acquaintance. In other words,' she stressed cruelly, 'you're yesterday's news and consequently stale. Now will you please leave and . . .'

Her voice ceased abruptly when he stepped towards her, his face a taut mask of fury. A flicker of fear gripped her throat when his hands—the well-shaped hands with the tapering fingers she had once loved—circled it and pressed lightly on her windpipe. His eyes held a cold savagery she had never seen before, and she flinched under their raking inspection of her features. This wasn't the Benedict she had known, loved . . . it was a stranger with a frightening tautness about him, a man perhaps unhinged by the sudden death of his wife only a week ago. Her eyes went down to the sardonic twist of his mouth, the white area around it betraying the tenseness coiled inside his lean body.

'So I'm yesterday's news, am I?' he said softly, his gaze settling at last on the faint tremble in her lower lip, parted slightly from the upper as real fear shivered over her skin. Dear God, he *was* mad, and she hadn't realised it! The pressure of his fingers on her throat would make sure any scream would be cut off at source, and she was no match for him physically. She stared dumbly into the glinting grey depths of his eyes and knew that he intended to kill her. Oddly, the conviction brought a kind of peace, as if fate had come full circle in its inexorable course.

She was incapable of speech, even when one of his hands lifted from her throat and his fingers ran lightly across the fullness of her lips, like a blind man haltingly reading Braille. Tension fled from her, to be replaced by a tingle of erotic excitement that bothered her far more than the thought of death had.

'Let's just see how stale I am to you,' he muttered, his head bending to take the place of his fingers with his mouth, his hand sliding slickly over the silk of her robe to press against her spine until her body touched his. Her moan of protest died in the throat he was now caressing with calculated sensitivity, even as his lips moved with the same purpose to rouse the demons of desire she had long ago put to rest.

Turgid warmth began an upward spiral from her loins to spread with slow intensity to every part of her body, to her firming breasts, to her toes, to the fingertips raised defensively against the smooth silk of his lapels. But there was little resistance when his lips grew hard and sought to part the curving tenderness of hers, draining her of every coherent thought except the deep need to release the tension building in her like dry tinder responding to the lick of flame.

Still some flicker of remembered pain made her moan against his lips when his hands fumbled to reach the shoulders of her robe, 'No! Please, no ...' Even that small protest died away when the robe fell from her shoulders to her waist, where it lodged between their joined hips and thighs. Her eyes closed on the surge of erotic pleasure that rippled and flowed through her when his hands stroked the firm points of her breasts then moulded the soft flesh to his palms. His thigh pressed insistently between hers until they parted in sudden yielding, and his breath deepened raggedly as his mouth covered the soft flesh of her neck close to the curved shell of her ear.

'Oh God, Serena,' he whispered, muffled, 'I've wanted you so much!'

Perhaps if he hadn't voiced words that made her brain lurch slowly into action again, she might have gone on being guided by instincts she had long ago buried. Or perhaps it was the sharp wail of his child from the next suite that brought her dizzily back to the reality of what was happening. Where moments ago her hands had unashamedly found their way under his jacket, under the crisp white shirt to caress the heated curves of his smoothly muscled chest, now she drew back, sick waves of horror taking the place of mindless ecstasy.

Her fingers defied her efforts to tie the sash of

her robe once she had shrugged it on to her shoulders again, and she turned her back on him, gritting, 'You've proved a point, Benedict, even if it wasn't the one you were thinking of. I'm woman enough to respond when a man forces himself on me, but that doesn't mean one damn thing, so don't go imagining I've been spending six years longing for the day when you'd come back into my life!'

He was silent for a moment or two, ignoring the plaintive calls from the small bedroom next door. Then, 'I didn't force myself on you, Serena,' he said hoarsely, 'and you know it. What happened between us before is something that couldn't be avoided, it wasn't right that we should be together then.'

'And now it is?' The belt now securely held at her waist, she swung round to throw him a contemptuous look. 'Now that your stepping-stone to the pinnacle of power is dead? Men like you make me sick!' she flailed with bitter weariness as another volley of cries came from the child next door. She threw up her hands in a gesture of disgust and said, 'Oh, go and see to your child before she wakes the whole place up. And be sure, Benedict,' she warned caustically, 'that as soon as I can find alternative accommodation for you and your—daughter, you'll be out of Windfair and out of my life for ever.'

The last words made her previous statement that he was yesterday's news a moot point, but she didn't recognise that fact until Benedict had walked out without a parting shot, his face an object lesson in taut control.

She stood unmoving, listening against her will to the child's gradually diminishing sobs until finally quiet reigned over Windfair's bedroom floor. Only then did she move to replace the robe with an equally silky low-necked nightdress before sliding into bed, rising again immediately to pad across the floor in bare feet to secure the door against further entry. Savagely, she hoped Benedict had heard the decisive click of the lock as she turned the previously unused key. After a moment's hesitation, she did the same with her sitting room door and returned to bed.

Not to sleep ... her body was too alert to the signs of passionate arousal to dissipate so rapidly. The tender fullness in her breasts testified to the extend of that arousal, and she muttered, 'Damn, damn, damn,' through her teeth as she punched her pillows into a more receptive cradle for the head that still had damp hair matted to its crown.

God, how she hated him ... hated the way he had calmly walked back into the schooled perfection of her life. He belonged to the past, why hadn't he stayed there? The response he had dredged from her tonight belonged truly to David ... David. A sharp twinge of longing pierced her for his sane normality, devoid of the dark passions that motivated Benedict.

The moon, tropical in size and brilliance, flooded into the room she had forgotten to curtain. Her thoughts darted around with the same fluidity as the moon's fitful light ebbed and waned with the passage of shady clouds over the night sky. Why had Benedict come here, with the daughter whose existence she hadn't even guessed at? A child whose eyes, so like Benedict's, reflected a sorrow too intense for her age. She was eight ... a bare two years old when Benedict had met

Serena in the café that night. Had he gone back to his loving father role, loving husband role, that next weekend when she had been weaving impossible dreams round his aura of sophistication mingled with his air of being at one with Chelsea's artistic element? How foolish she had been, how unutterably naïve, to believe that her love could make a difference in his life. That he could become a successful writer with her encouragement and support. And all the time he had been living a double life, secure with the wife who guaranteed a swift rise to the top of his profession . . . banking.

It took no effort of imagination to visualise his suitably modest acceptance of a place on the board, his assured progress to Chairman when his father-in-law retired. Wasn't that what he had worked so long and so hard to achieve? Power could be heady, she acknowledged, and Benedict was the man to carry it off with ease. It wouldn't matter to him that the daughter who clung so desperately to him was obviously a candidate for a psychiatrist's couch in later years.

The silence prevailing in the adjoining suite proved that Benedict was a good father . . . didn't it? The child with haunted eyes clung blindly to him, was comforted by the mere fact of his presence. Yet Serena drew back mentally and emotionally from the seeming rapport between father and daughter. Wasn't it possible that the child clung to him for the very obvious reason that he was all she had left in a bewildering world made hostile by the death of her mother?

It was all too fraught with emotional overtones Serena felt herself unable to handle. Only one certainty filled her mind as she dropped finally into sleep ... Benedict and his daughter would have to go at the earliest possible moment.

Despatching Benedict and his daughter proved just as difficult practically as it did emotionally. Even Clive had not appeared for his Sunday stint of duty when Serena lifted the phone at the reception desk.

'Hello, Denise? Sorry to disturb you so early, but I have a problem. There's a man and his eight-year-old daughter staying here, and I think they'd be much happier with you. You have children she could play with——'

'Sorry, my dear,' Denise returned, only a huskiness in her voice betraying the fact that she had been wakened from a well-deserved sleep. 'We're absolutely filled to the rafters this week with the yachting fraternity. To tell the truth, I'd appreciate some non-seagoing guests at the moment,' she confessed with wry amusement, 'but bookings are bookings with us at this time of the year. I'd have thought it was the same with you?' she queried curiously.

'Yes, of course,' Serena returned quickly. 'It's just that Windfair isn't exactly geared to children of her age. I thought she'd be happier with younger people.'

'Mmm. Well, you can try the Crofts,' Denise suggested doubtfully, 'although Margo was boasting to me only yesterday that they're fully booked until next week. Still, you could try her.'

'Yes. Thanks, Denise,' Serena rang off with a sense of fatalism. If Denise with her own brood of four children could find no room for Benedict and his daughter, there was little likelihood that space would be found for them in any other small guesthouse. She stared broodingly at the handsome staircase that led to the upper floor. Her request for accommodation would meet with similar discouragement from the other guesthouses on the island. Yachting events attracted the international set to Bermuda's sunny shores, and Serena was as helpless as Clive had been in securing alternative accommodation for Benedict and his daughter.

What a disturbing child she was, Serena mused as she turned her head to look at the dawn's sunny glow touching the tips of the trees surrounding Windfair. The humblest of Bermuda's inhabitants would have been ashamed to dress a child in the haphazard style Benedict's daughter had appeared in yesterday, the pale salmon dress stealing what animation she possessed and her hair a challenge even to Matty's skilled ministrations. What sort of woman had Caroline Ramsay been? Evidently a self-centred beauty uncaring of her small daughter's appearance.

Yet ... suppose Caroline had had some slow-growing illness which eventually claimed her life? Could she blame Benedict for sticking by the woman he had married? But what illness could linger on for years, as Caroline's would have to? Most of the dread diseases had a short and stormy history. None that she knew of would merit Benedict's unswerving loyalty to the woman he had married and created a child with, not for so many years.

Serena caught up her wandering thoughts, her mouth compressing into a narrow line. What in God's name was she trying to do—justify Benedict's actions six years ago? Excuse her own response to his lovemaking last night? It would make a lovely story, she mocked herself silently, dramatic too. True love blossoming in the midst of turmoil ... wife's fatal illness forcing husband to turn elsewhere for the affection denied because of his wife's affliction. Plausible in a sentimental novel, ridiculous in the light of reality. Proof of that leapt out of the grey eyes of his daughter, proof of the love that had existed between Benedict and his wife. And he had the gall to come here now and ...

'Why are you up so early?' demanded Matty querulously as she walked with heavy tread across the hall and drew up at the reception desk with a baleful look at the girl she had cared for from birth. Her habit was to begin Serena's day with the hot fragrant tea she brought on a tray to her bedside, and seeing her charge independently up and functioning on her own obviously didn't sit well on her. 'I was just about to bring you a tray,' she challenged belligerently, dark liquid eyes affronted as they took in Serena's state of dress in white shirtwaister dress and hair-style that took time to fix.

'I had to make a few telephone calls,' Serena informed her curtly, wondering why she bothered to explain to the temperamental housekeeper, who would disdain this disruption to her routine whatever the reason.

'At this time of the day?' Matty's eyes rolled significantly in the direction of the broad windows where the sun was only now touching the panes with its red-gold fingers of light. 'Nobody in the world is up this early, Miss Serena, except for me coming to light the stove and make your tea.'

Ignoring the reproach subtly conveyed, Serena glanced down at the desk top as if important missives lay there for her attention. Damn, why should she cater to the old woman who bounded her existence by Windfair's perimeters? Yet, sighing, she knew that Matty would demand, probe, uncover the reasons for her charge's presence at the desk before the sun had reached the middle pane on the hall windows. 'Mrs Acton at Seaspray always rises early, and I called her to find out if she could accommodate Mr—Ramsey and his daughter for the duration of their stay on Bermuda. The girl,' she added sternly against Matty's quivering objection, 'needs other children to play with.'

'That child,' Matty snorted forcefully, 'needs a loving mother, not children to pass the time of day with. She hangs like a leech to her daddy, but it's her mother she needs. The mother she lost last week, Miss Serena,' the older woman reproached, 'and here you are threatening to throw her out to anyone who'll catch her!'

'I am not throwing her out,' Serena retorted through her teeth. 'I simply think she'll get over her mother's death more quickly if she has other children to interest her. Now will you please allow me to make arrangements I think will be suitable for her?'

Matty drew up her vast bosom into dignified disdain. 'Whatever you think, Miss Serena,' she acquiesced in her most remote voice, spoiling the effect by muttering audibly as she went majestically towards the kitchen, 'Thank the good Lord that Mr Charles didn't throw you out the way you're intending to abandon that poor child!'

Serena sighed again, drawing a deep breath that expelled itself on unbidden memories of Matty's cushiony bosom receiving the hurts and woes of her own childhood. Which Matty had intended, she reflected sourly, wondering abstractly why the black woman possessed such a rapport with the tender feelings of children when she had none of her own. Only the undying loyalty of the one she had succoured selflessly through all the long years of growing up. It was for Matty's sake, not Benedict's or his daughter's, that Serena gave up on her efforts to find other accommodation for them. But be it on Matty's head to keep both of them out of her way for the next two weeks!

And it worked ... for a few days at least.

CHAPTER SIX

BENEDICT might have been any other father indulging a small daughter. As if Serena had never existed for him, he devoted himself to showing Debra the sights of Bermuda.

Debra ... that was her name. Debra ... Deborah. She grew more eloquent with each day that passed, excitedly relaying to an interested Matty, who always seemed to be hovering in the hall on their return, the highlights of whatever new sight they had seen that day.

'I fed the fish at—what was the name of the place, Daddy?'

Benedict's eyes, a faint trace of mockery in their depths, met Serena's as he answered his daughter's question. 'Devil's Hole.'

'Yes, and then we ...' The child chattered on to the flatteringly interested Matty, but Serena found it impossible to draw her gaze away from Benedict's, as if a silken thread bound them together. Already he looked a different man, the sallowness underlying his slightly olive skin disappearing under the unpolluted rays of Bermuda's sun; he had apparently taken to the shorts habitually worn by the men of Bermuda whether at work or play; his sinewy lean arms in short-sleeved shirts quickly recovered the tan of earlier years.

She became aware that Matty was looking at her strangely, evidently having said something to her more than once. Was there a gleam of triumph in Benedict's eyes when she withdrew her own? 'I'm sorry, Matty, did you say something to me?' She was standing behind the reception desk relieving Pat who had taken her tea break, and her fingers tightened whitely on the smooth wood.

'Miss Debra is interested in painting, and I told her you'd let her see yours in the cottage,' Matty repeated, beaming her pride in Serena's work.

'Miss Debra' indeed! Serena fumed inwardly, although her exterior remained calm, almost cold. It was due solely to the elderly housekeeper's efforts that the child no longer looked like a reject from a badly run orphanage. This past day or two her brown hair had been neatly plaited and boasted a knife-edged straightness in its centre parting which could only be Matty's work. The unbecoming salmon dress hadn't been seen since that first afternoon; instead, shorts and tops had become the order of the day with pretty floral dresses for late afternoon, probably with Matty's connivance also.

'I'm afraid it's not convenient at the moment,' Serena said coolly, smiling to a pair of returning guests and wishing they would come across and enquire about something.

'We can wait,' Benedict returned blandly, laying a lean-fingered hand on his daughter's head, 'can't we, poppet?'

The child's grey eyes, so like her father's, stared for a moment into Serena's. On the few occasions when they had run into each other unavoidably, the girl had seemed to shrink away from Serena. Irritating, but then she had no wish to cultivate a liking for Benedict's daughter ... Caroline's daughter.

'I don't think she wants us to see her paintings, Daddy.'

What a perspicacious child!

'Of course Miss Serena wants you to see them,' intervened Matty. 'People from all over the world buy her paintings, because they want to remember Bermuda when they go back to their own place. She's the best painter of Bermuda there is.'

Benedict gave Serena an oddly intense look before looking down at his daughter. 'Why don't we go and have some tea, and then perhaps Miss Howard will be free to show us some of her artwork? All right with you, Miss Howard, if we come back in half an hour or so?'

Without seeming completely uncivilised, Serena had no choice but to nod her head ungraciously, and she turned furiously on Matty when the other two sauntered off hand in hand.

'What are you thinking of, Matty?' she demanded hotly. 'You know I don't like people poking around in my studio.'

'I thought you'd changed your mind about that, since you took Mr Storey's guests down there last week,' Matty replied with an innocent rounding of her eyes which didn't fool Serena for a moment.

'That was different altogether,' she snapped. 'Mr and Mrs Allen bought the painting I'd just finished.'

'Well, maybe Mr Ramsey will take a fancy to the one you're working on now.' Tongue in cheek, Matty swayed away down the hall and Serena glared after her resentfully, thinking dire thoughts of retirement for the old housekeeper on the far side of the island.

Her voice was crisp when she answered the

telephone a moment later, and David said, 'Oh-oh, it sounds as if you're in the same kind of stew I'm in at the moment. Are you free to talk for a minute?' He had no way of knowing that Serena's mind went blank at the sound of his voice, that she stared far off into space while her fingers tightened on the receiver held to her ear. How could she—possibly—have forgotten David's existence for the past few days?

'Hello, Serena? Are you there?'

'Yes, David, I'm here.'

'Sorry I haven't been in touch, but it's been hell around here. Wrong booking, changed bookings, no bookings at all. In fact, I'm phoning you now to see if you can put up a couple and their eighteen-year-old son for a week. His secretary got the dates wrong, and I haven't even a rafter to swing them on.'

'No, I——' Serena began, then her brain moved into high gear. 'Yes, as a matter of fact, I can, David. They can have my suite and I'll use the cottage.' At least that way it would be much easier to put Benedict out of her mind ... difficult when only the thickness of a wall separated their beds.

David demurred, as she knew he would, but he finally accepted her offer gratefully. 'Thanks, Serena. Your kindness makes it very difficult for me to say what I'm going to next,' he sounded rueful.

'You've found another woman and you'd rather marry her,' she quipped, one eye beginning to watch the dining room doors for Benedict's return.

David laughed. 'Wish it was as clearcut as that! No, the fact is that the boating fraternity staying here are planning a shindig on Saturday night and they want me to attend. As it isn't an affair I think you'd enjoy. . . .'

'I get the message,' she said lightly. 'Our dinner has to be postponed, right? Don't worry, David, I have plenty to occupy me here. Enjoy yourself.'

'You're a most unusual woman,' he said huskily, 'and I love you.'

She began a wrestle with guilt after replacing the receiver, unsure of why she had said there was plenty to do here on Saturday night. There was nothing, apart from another solitary dinner in her office. She had avoided the dining room these past days, knowing Benedict would be at his table inside the doors, perhaps coming over to join her unasked, knowing she wouldn't create a scene in front of a room full of her paying guests. She had no wish to talk to him, to hear his no doubt plausible excuses for his behaviour six years ago. It had taken a toll on her heart to get over him once, without the added problem of what to believe or not to believe which he would present now.

Her expression brightened at the moment when Benedict and his daughter emerged from the dining room. Of course! On Saturday night she would be safely installed in the cottage, sealed off from staff and guests inhabiting Windfair.

Benedict gave her a sharp look as he approached, and Serena sobered her expression. It wouldn't do for him to think that his presence gave her any joy whatsoever, which was exactly his conclusion, she could tell.

Pat came hurrying up behind them and reached the desk first. 'Sorry to have taken so long, but I couldn't hurry away too rudely from the people I was talking to.'

'No problem. If you need me, I'll be in the cottage.' Serena stepped from behind reception and nodded briskly to Benedict, ignoring the small girl who again levelled her disconcerting stare at her. 'If you'd like to come with me, I'll take you down to my studio.' Before he had time to answer, she set a brisk pace for the side door letting out on to the dining terrace and let it fall back into Benedict's hand as she crossed the flagstones to the steps leading down to the gardens.

Like a tour guide, she kept her tone impersonal as she pointed to various features of the gardens. 'The gazebo over there was erected by Peregrine Howard for his wife, Matilda, who found Bermuda's heat oppressive at times. She could watch her children at play while she herself appreciated the shade provided by the summer-house. Most of the trees have been here for many years, some of them planted by Peregrine himself. For a seagoing man, he was remarkably ...' Her eye fell on the child struggling to keep up with her rapid pace, and the words faded when she saw the awed look in Debra's light grey eyes. She knew little about children, but she could well remember the feeling of crass boredom when adults spouted off unintelligibly.

'A path winds through these woods,' she altered her voice scarcely at all, 'and it leads to an enchanted cottage. There are roses round the door planted, they say, by a beautiful princess who was spirited to Bermuda on the orders of a wicked stepmother jealous of her beauty, which far outshone her own daughter's.' Debra stumbled on the path they were just entering, too absorbed in what Serena was saying to notice the tree root in her way. Benedict was silent as he walked beside her, but she knew he was listening too, probably astounded by her abrupt change of face, as she herself was.

'Go on, Miss Howard,' Debra breathed, 'what happened to the princess?'

'Well, she planted the root of a rose she'd managed to pluck from the palace grounds as she was taken away, knowing that the prince would recognise it when he sailed the seven seas searching for her. It was a rose that had special meaning for them, its heart red for love and its petals shading to white to signify purity.'

'And did the prince see the rose and find her?'

'Yes. He sailed the seas and looked for her everywhere, and just when he was about to give up he came ashore on Bermuda and walked among the beautiful flowers he found there. But none was as beautiful as the rose with the red heart and white petals, because he knew that inside the cottage he would find his princess. Perhaps you can see the cottage and the roses if you go ahead a little.'

'That was nice of you,' Benedict said quietly when Debra went eagerly towards the next bend in the path. 'She—hasn't known much of enchantment in her short life.' He paused. 'Tell me, will she find roses with red hearts for love and white petals for purity growing round your cottage door?'

CHAPTER SEVEN

'OH, yes,' Serena returned to crispness, 'there are roses growing round my cottage door, but the connotation is strictly fairytale invention. I hope your daughter won't take it too much to heart, because as we all know, life doesn't offer too many happy fairytale endings.'

'You're still very bitter, aren't you?' Benedict asked, his voice pitched low, 'yet you won't give me a hearing to explain . . .'

'Explain!' Serena halted abruptly and swivelled round on the powdery earth marking the path, her eyes sparking sea-green fury. 'Can't you understand that I'm not interested in hearing explanations for what happened six years ago! And even if I had the slightest interest, I wouldn't believe you! Why should I trust you now when I couldn't then?' She drew a deep, quivering breath. 'There is just one thing I'd be interested in hearing, Benedict, and that's your real reason for coming here with your daughter. What in God's name did you hope to accomplish?'

His face had paled under the beginning tan, but his eyes matched the anger in hers. 'Perhaps I wanted to see how well my investment is doing,' he bit off shortly.

'Your—what?' Serena could feel the colour drain from her face as she stared up into his stormy eyes. Instinct told her he meant an investment in Windfair, but—how, why? She turned

dazedly to look at Debra as she came running
back along the path, shouting excitedly to
Benedict.

'I found it, Daddy, I found it! . . . the enchanted
cottage! Come and see.' She tugged at his hand and
looked up into his face, and what she saw there made
her smile falter, the grey eyes so like his turning on
Serena accusingly. 'What did you say to my daddy?
Oh, I hate you, hate you . . .!' She ran off blindly,
sobbing, back towards the house, oblivious to
Benedict's sharp call for her to return.

'I'll have to go after her,' he said without
looking at Serena, and she knew he blamed her for
the child's upset, but she was too numb with shock
to worry about that unfairness. Then he did look
back at her, his eyes coldly bitter. 'You agree we
have to talk?'

Serena nodded, staring at him speechless.

'Then stay here, I'll be back.' He was already
loping off along the winding path when she found
her voice.

'Matty will take care of her.'

Serena didn't know whether he'd heard her or
not, but she turned automatically towards the
cottage, the roses she had spun into her fantasy
shimmering with an iridescent glow she was
scarcely aware of as she took the key from under
the geranium pot and opened the door. Leaving it
open, she walked numbly to the big armchair
which had been her father's, and dropped into it to
stare unseeingly through the window where vines
rioted over the high fences in a cascade of colour.

What had he meant—his investment? David had
arranged the loans for Windfair's renovations from
his bank. She would never have been able to

obtain such a large sum on her own. With the best will in the world, no bank would put faith in a commercially inexperienced twenty-one-year-old. But if Benedict had put up the money, why hadn't David told her so instead of letting her think that he had pulled every string he had to get the bank to agree to the loan?

She felt sick, as if every prop that supported her had been suddenly pulled out from under her. *Why hadn't David told her?* For that matter, why hadn't Benedict? Each of them had cheated her in his own way—David for taking credit where none was due, and Benedict for neglecting to give her an option as to whether or not she would accept a loan from him. Which, considering the circumstances, she would have refused categorically.

And she would have lost Windfair, a voice whispered remindingly in her head. But, dear God, wouldn't that have been better than being beholden to Benedict until the loan was paid off? Her thoughts turned painfully to his reasons for advancing the money in the first place. Conscience payment? She was sure that seducing virgins wasn't one of his many faults, and she had been partly to blame there because she hadn't made it clear that he would be the first for her.

She didn't hear Benedict come in, but she felt no surprise when she looked back into the room and saw him standing close to the left arm of her chair.

'Debra?'

He nodded tersely. 'She's with Matty.'

'Why did you put up the money for Windfair?' she asked dully.

'Would you have preferred a developer to get his hands on it?'

'I would have preferred to have a choice in the matter.'

Benedict shrugged, and turned away to walk to the small table, picking up one of the two basket tub chairs in one hand and carrying it over to place it so that his back was to the window wall.

'Was it conscience money?' she asked tautly as he dropped into the seat and leaned forward to balance an elbow on each knee, his hands clasped loosely between them.

'Partly, I suppose,' he lifted one brow as if the idea was new to him. 'Crashing in where no other man had dared to tread wasn't my scene, then or now. Believe it or not, I'd never been unfaithful to Caroline before. I'd wanted to a few times,' he went on with brutal frankness, ignoring her flinch, 'but until you it had never seemed worth the subterfuge involved. And it needed a lot of that in order to go on seeing you. I knew it was madness, and yet I had to see you—no, don't say anything yet,' he said tersely when she opened her mouth to speak. 'Let me give you the whole picture before you make a judgment.'

She had made that judgment long ago and nothing he could say now would alter it. Nevertheless she sat back in her chair and regarded him stonily, still shaken by the knowledge that he had advanced the loan for Windfair.

'Caroline was what's known in psychiatric jargon as a paranoid schizophrenic,' he resumed, speaking so matter-of-factly that the words only belatedly penetrated Serena's consciousness. Then her body tensed as if to ward off further blows. She didn't want to hear this, to dredge up sorrow for a woman she had once hated. 'She had been diagnosed as being mentally disturbed long before we met, but I wasn't told about it. Her father believed that psychiatry was nonsense, that if he ignored the problem it would go away.' For the first time his tone was coloured with grey bitterness.

'I went into the bank straight from university, as green as they come and twice as ambitious. I was flattered when Sir Harold invited me to his London house and to weekends at his country place. Naturally I met Caroline, his beautiful daughter, and fell in love with her. I couldn't believe my luck when Sir Harold encouraged me to ask her to marry me.' One hand rose and clamped round his mouth as if to cover its trembling, and Serena broke her silence involuntarily.

'Benedict, don't! Don't tell me this, please.' Whether for his sake or her own she didn't want to hear more. Like a completed jigsaw puzzle suddenly shattering into unrelated pieces, her preconceived notions were crumbling into frightening disorder.

'I have to, Serena,' he said, composed again. 'Don't you see that? Whatever the outcome I have to tell you the true facts of what was happening six years ago, why I—deceived you.' She made no further response, so he went on, 'If I'd known more about her illness then, I'd have recognised certain symptoms—the tantrums when she thought I so much as glanced at another woman, the over-abject penitence when I convinced her there was no truth to her suspicions. It was after—Debra was born that her illness blossomed into full-blown schizophrenia. I'm not going into all the details,' he dismissed starkly, 'but fortunately her paranoia was centred on me, not Debra.

'Can you wonder that you, with all your vibrant eagerness to grasp life and shake it by the tail, became like a drug to me? You were so sane, so normal ... you made me feel like the young man I'd never really been. It wasn't fair to you, but I had to go on seeing you. You were the one lifeline to sanity, you and——' He paused. 'I suppose I should clear all the decks,' he resumed almost diffidently. 'Chisholm Cottage wasn't a place I shared with a writer. Although I suppose in a way I did. That part of my life was an escape valve from the rest of it.'

Serena's brain, still reeling from the shock of what he had told her, only slowly made his meaning clear. 'You mean—*you* were writing there?'

'Yes ... fortunately in a successful way.' Benedict got to his feet and came to stand over her. 'So don't go on thinking that the money for Windfair came from or through my wife.'

He had known she would think that, and hate it for that reason. But at this moment she wasn't sure if Benedict's own money wasn't just as objectionable.

Her hands came up to cover her face, and she said, muffled, through them, 'Leave me alone, Benedict ... please.' There was too much to think of all at once, too many loose ends waiting to be tied. Her hands came down from her face as he reached the door. 'Benedict?' she said tightly.

'Yes?'

'How did Caroline die?'

Even across the room's distance she could see the bleak shadow descend again over his eyes. 'She killed herself,' he said starkly, and was gone.

*   *   *

Serena stayed in her chair until long after the sun had set and shadows became night. Too many questions had been answered, and too many remained unanswered. If Caroline was as sick as he had told her she was, why had he left their daughter in her care? Surely her illness might have veered to encompass even the child? And why had Benedict himself remained married to her when it would have been better for everyone concerned if he had put her into competent medical care and divorced her? *If what he had told her was true.*

Oh God, she didn't know what to think! Her fingers rose to massage temples that were beginning to throb. Given time, she could check the truth or otherwise of his statements—but then perhaps not, if Caroline's father, Sir Harold, still refused to acknowledge that his daughter suffered from a grave mental illness. Would any father so callously ignore a condition that required treatment in his child?

Her thoughts wove to and fro until she felt disorientated herself. There was one way she could verify one part of what Benedict had told her— David. She would know, even across a telephone line, if he had lied to her about his part in providing the money for Windfair. Moving quickly, she walked through the darkened cottage and locked the door behind her. The path up to the house was only barely visible, but her feet were sure as they walked rapidly along its twisting curves.

Lights from the dining terrace cast a flickering glow across the lawn, and Serena chose the side door into the hall, relieved to find Clive its only occupant. 'Get Mr Storey of Moongate on the telephone for me, would you, please? And put it through to my suite.'

Ten minutes passed before the phone rang, and she leapt to answer it. 'David?'

'They're still trying to find him, Miss Howard,' Clive's voice came through instead, 'but he should——'

'Storey here,' David cut briskly across the line, and Serena heard the click as Clive disengaged from the call.

'David, it's me, Serena. You sound terribly busy, but I have to talk to you.' It occurred to her suddenly that posing her question over the telephone when he was harried wouldn't accomplish her purpose. She had to see him face to face, note his reaction. 'Could you possibly come over?'

'*Now?*' David blurted out the astounded word without thinking, only belatedly remembering that it was his fiancée he was speaking to, and that she seldom—never—called him to come and see her on short notice. 'Is it important, darling? Is there a problem with the Carter family?'

She stared blankly at the expensive paper covering the wall in front of her. Who on earth were the Carter family? Suddenly she remembered agreeing to give up her suite for the people who were booked for a later date at Moongate. 'Er . . . no, there's no problem there. When will they be arriving?' She hoped there would be time to clear her personal effects and clothing from the suite by the time the unexpected visitors arrived.

'I'm surprised they're not there already,' David returned worriedly. 'They said they'd get settled in at Windfair and have dinner there.'

'No problem. I'll go down and see if they've arrived.'

'Serena?'

'Yes?' Her voice was as clipped as his own had been on announcing himself on the telephone.

'If you really need to see me tonight, I can perhaps get over later?'

'Oh. No . . . no, it's all right, David. Tomorrow will do.' She would be too busy in the next little while organising the Carters to think of the reason why she had wanted to see David.

The door to the bedroom of the next suite was open as she hurried by, and she caught a glimpse of Matty in the alcove bedroom beyond. Backtracking, she called, 'Matty, I need you,' and as the older woman ambled towards the door, continued, 'There's a family of three arriving any moment to occupy my rooms. Can you make them ready, and see that there's a cot set up in the sitting room for the teenage son?'

Matty loved situations that called for emergency action, but now her plump face was troubled as she looked back into the suite behind her. 'Well, I promised Mr Ramsey I'd stay with his little girl,' she said softly.

Serena gave her a frosty look. 'Then perhaps you'd better find Mr Ramsey and ask him to take care of his daughter himself, because I need you at the moment.'

'I think he went out somewhere,' Matty volunteered worriedly.

'Then find someone else who can see to my suite,' snapped Serena, fuming as she went towards the staircase. How dared he tear her life apart and then walk out as if he had only himself

to consider! And using Matty like a nanny in a
private house he had deigned to visit with his
daughter!

The frown disappeared from her brow when she
saw the group clustered round the reception desk,
Clive's face clouded with embarrassment as he
looked down at the bookings register, not for the
first time, she suspected.

'I'm sorry, Mr Carter,' he looked up as Serena
approached, 'there must be some mistake. I have
no record of your booking.'

A florid-faced man in his forties, flanked by a
plumply fair woman and a bored-looking sixteen-
or seventeen-year-old boy, said aggressively, 'I
don't care if the name Carter isn't written in your
damn register, we've been sent here by Mr Storey
of the Moongate Inn. What a bloody place!' he
raged to no one in particular. 'I'll take my business
to the Bahamas again next year—at least they
know who I am!'

'I'm sure they will, Mr Carter,' Serena intervened
coolly, 'if your secretary in London collects her
wits enough to book you in for the correct dates.'

He swung round, his ruddy complexion turning
a deeper shade of red when he noted Serena's
aristocratic bearing. 'What?'

'I'm Serena Howard,' she told him without
extending her hand as would have been normal. 'Mr
Storey telephoned me to ask if I could accommodate
you for this week, which your secretary had left in
limbo, and I agreed to accept you and your family.'
She turned with a tight smile to Clive, who seemed
paralysed by the other man's aggressiveness. 'I'm
sorry, Clive, I should have made a note of Mr
Storey's request, but it was on very short notice.'

'That's all right, Miss Howard,' he said seriously. 'Shall I see Mr and Mrs Carter to their room?'

'*Room!*' Carter's voice recovered volume. 'We were told we'd have a suite—although,' he glanced disparagingly round the ancient hall, 'I doubt if a guesthouse runs to decent accommodation.'

Serena stifled the retort that rose to mind; she hadn't received many guests of Carter's type, but those she had had convinced her of the futility of argument.

'You have a suite, Mr Carter, although I'm afraid at such short notice it's not quite ready for you yet. However, by the time you've had dinner in our excellent dining room, everything will be ready for you. Clive, would you see that the luggage is taken up to Suite Six? If you'd like to come with me,' she invited the Carters, who forged ahead of her, 'I'll take you to the dining room. Our chefs are well known internationally . . .' She managed to give Clive a wry wink as she led her reluctant charges away, and after a moment's stunned reaction, he grinned and stared admiringly after her.

When, finally, Serena closed the cottage door behind her, she heaved a heartfelt sigh. No one could reach her here unless they came on foot, and only a dire emergency would bring anyone to invade the privacy of her studio. Her head throbbed with a dull ache, and she went into the tiny bathroom to take aspirin from the medicine chest and wash three tablets down with water.

The Carters had proved even more horrendous on better acquaintance. Frank, the patriarch, had complained about the food, the accommodation, the possible misfunction of the plumbing in such an old house. Lance, the son, had deplored the lack of entertainment in a morosely sulky way. She should have a disco, he told Serena patronisingly, and she'd attract more business to the house which, in his eyes, was crumbling into obscurity. Only Sandra, the wife and mother, made no direct complaints, although she looked with misgivings on the cot bed set up in the living room for her son.

'Lance won't like this,' she confided worriedly. 'He's used to his independence, you see, and he won't like it that his dad and I can hear him come and go. He's very sensitive, is Lance—you know, he hates little animals being chopped up to make fur coats, I had to throw all mine out when he got in with this conservation group,' she pronounced slowly. 'Hates anything unnatural, does Lance. None of his girl-friends wears make-up, you know, but then they can take that, can't they, being young?'

Serena now put the foolish chatter out of her mind, not disliking Sandra Carter as much as feeling pity for her. What a horrendous existence it must be, married to a martinet, possessing a son like Lance. She went back into the large room and her gaze was drawn to the painting propped on the easel she used for current work. There was nothing Matty would like about this picture; no quaint Bermuda lanes, cottages, harbour scenes. It was violent, of no conventional shape or form, colour exploding in bursts of cerise, orange, harsh yellow, then the cooler shades of violet, blue, green. It was an unbalanced picture, one she had painted in a trancelike state so that she scarcely remembered laying down one brush and picking up another.

Unbalanced ... the way she had felt since Benedict came back into her life, stirring up the old passions she had thought were dead. With a sudden movement, she picked up a muslin drape and threw it over the canvas that reflected so accurately the state of her own emotions, then coiled herself into the capacious old leather chair. The one Benedict had used was still by the window opposite, and she seemed to see his lean figure still there, elbows on knees, long forearms darkly clouded with short curling hair. Strange that she remembered that small detail about him when his face remained obscure. But then the light had been behind him, shadows of late afternoon obscuring his expression.

Was that something he had planned so that she couldn't be sure whether or not he spoke the truth? There was no doubt in her mind that Caroline was dead ... not even Benedict could conjure up the stark emotion his voice had held when he said, 'She killed herself.'

But why had she been driven to take her own life—*why*? Was it because, as he had said, Caroline was mentally ill and put an end to the life she could no longer bear? Or—Serena let her head fall back against the corner of the chair and closed her eyes. Or had she finally realised that there would always be other women in Benedict's life as there had been in the past? Had she loved him so much that she could no longer accept that he remained married to her for one reason only—that his ambition might be fed from her father's storehouse?

'Oh God!' Serena gasped out loud, pain twisting inside her like a viable thing. Why had he come

back to torment her like this? She could give him
nothing . . . she had no love left for him, no trust,
nothing. The physical response he had drawn from
her was just that . . . physical, an involuntary
reaction to being reminded suddenly of a youthful
love affair that had made her happy for a time.

So why are you so wrought up over something
that means nothing any more? the treacherous
voice of reason whispered in her mind. She loved
David now, would marry him very soon, and
whatever was lacking of passion in their relationship now would be forgotten in the security of
David's love. Benedict had done that for her, she
thought bitterly . . . no man would ever take her to
his bed again until she was sure he was free to do
so.

She got up suddenly, unable to be still with her
thoughts any more, but when she lay in bed
minutes later they went relentlessly on. Had
Benedict spoken truth about his success as a
writer? That the loan for Windfair had come from
that source rather than through Caroline? She
would surely have seen books written by Benedict
Ramsey, although it was likely he used a
pseudonym if writing was, as he had said, a relief
from the horror of his life otherwise. Ironic that
she had urged him to try writing, and all the
time . . . Why had he been so secretive, even with
her, if it was true that she was the only one he'd
forsaken Caroline for?

At last, from sheer exhaustion, she slept.

In the morning, just before eight, Serena went into
the dining room and saw Matty at the Ramsey
table, coaxing Debra to sample the huge cooked

breakfast set before her. As Serena had done years before, the child balked at the amount of food she was expected to consume. There was no sign of Benedict at the table.

'Come along now, my deary,' Matty crooned, 'just try this lovely sausage. You want to grow up to be a strong healthy girl, don't you?'

Serena shook her head wryly. Matty was like a berserk woman who stole babies from prams outside shops to satisfy a thwarted maternal instinct. She went over to the table, conscious that Debra's grey eyes became immediately wary at her approach.

'Perhaps she doesn't want to be stuffed like a prize trout,' she intervened crisply.

'The child has to eat,' insisted Matty in her most stubborn voice, her eyes indicating that Serena's presence was far from welcome.

'But perhaps she'd prefer something else— maybe a mixed fresh fruit plate with a dressing of cream?'

A glint of interest showed momentarily in the grey eyes, then they took on a closed expression before Debra looked down again at the plate in front of her.

'She needs more than fruit to fill her up.' Matty was furious at having her authority usurped.

'Lunch is only four hours away,' Serena returned calmly, wondering at her own motives for siding with Benedict's child. 'Let her have what she wants now, and her father can decide on what she needs for lunch.'

Debra was a strange little creature, she reflected as she went to her special table in the corner. Half child, half—what? A look in her eyes sometimes suggested an adult who had glimpsed hell. Perhaps she had, living with a psychotic mother.

'Good morning, John,' she smiled to the day waiter attending her table. 'I'll have orange juice, and——' her gaze fell on Debra over by the door, 'fresh fruit with cream.'

'No eggs, Miss Howard?'

She shook her head, and he grinned as he went towards the kitchen. Matty thought of her as the eight-year-old Debra was, and would demand a full accounting of what Serena had begun her day with; fortunately, the younger members of the staff, like John, held the elderly housekeeper in little awe.

Where was Benedict? she wondered. Hadn't he returned from his night out? Her mouth tightened as she looked out to the dining terrace with its white metal tables and chairs and the potted plants that emphasised the tropic ambience of Windfair. There were always women available in Bermuda for men on the loose; jaded holidaymakers and bored wives, found in every resort area.

At that moment he came into the dining room, his body lines still tautly drawn in beige knee-length Bermuda shorts and coffee-coloured shirt, but his face bore traces of a night unwisely spent.

He stopped to have a few words with his daughter, who became instantly animated, and with Matty, who seemed no less enchanted. Debra's face fell when he patted her head and turned to walk towards Serena's table.

'May I join you?'

'I think your daughter might enjoy your company more,' she returned levelly.

'She's almost finished breakfast, and Matty is

taking her shopping at Trimingham's shortly.' He
pulled out the chair opposite and dropped into it,
spreading his elbows on the white cloth and giving
Serena an intent look from eyes that were faintly
red-rimmed. She was aware too of the dark swoop
of his brows above them, and the mouth that was
presently tautly drawn, but which could assume
the manipulative softness of passion when he
chose to exert that part of his nature. She had no
love for him, but she would have had to be a
woman of stone not to remember how it felt to be
kissed by those lips, held in those sinewy arms with
their virile spattering of dark curling hair.

She moistened her lips with the orange juice
John at that moment brought to her, looking away
towards the terrace again while Benedict ordered
his breakfast. A large tomato juice to counter the
effects of his night spree, eggs lightly scrambled,
black coffee.

'Matty is employed by me as housekeeper, not
as a child minder for the guests,' she remarked
tartly when John had glided out of earshot again.
'A girl can be found to take care of your
daughter, if you wish.'

'I don't wish,' he said shortly, then gave a harsh-
sounding sigh. 'Debra seems to have taken to
Matty in a way she seldom does with strangers,
and I don't want her upset again so soon
after ...' He stopped abruptly and nodded his
thanks to John for the rapid delivery of the large
glass of tomato juice. 'If you prefer, I'll pay for her
services or for someone to take over her house
duties for the time being.'

Serena's eyes widened in astonishment, then as
quickly narrowed as anger swept through her.

'Aren't you forgetting that as the owner of Windfair
I direct the staff where needed? I've managed
extremely well without your direction until now,
and I see no need to alter that state of affairs.' Her
fingers were trembling with tension, and she
replaced her glass on the table. Arrogance wasn't
one of the qualities she remembered in him, but
she was beginning to realise just how little she had
known him six years ago. She had been like an
exuberant puppy dancing slavishly around him,
too infatuated to see fault in him. But she was no
longer that naïve girl; she was a woman who had
worked her way through a particularly harassing
mill to the security she knew today.

'Aren't *you* forgetting,' Benedict leaned across
the table to say softly, 'that I have quite a
substantial interest in Windfair?'

Bright spots of anger mottled Serena's cheek-
bones. 'Are you suggesting that your money
bought you a say in Windfair's management?'

He shrugged. 'Aren't investors usually concerned
about what happens to their capital?' he countered,
casual as he took a long draught of the juice in his
glass. His gaze was caught by a movement at the far
side of the room, and he raised a lazy hand to wave
to his daughter and Matty, who were leaving their
table with, from Debra at least, wistful glances in
Benedict's direction. But at her farther's gesture, she
quite happily tucked a hand into Matty's brown
plump one and went willingly out into the hall, both
obviously intent on their shopping expedition.

'I've checked my financial position this morning,' Serena said tightly, 'and find that it's possible
to pay back the loan you advanced, so you need
worry no further about your investment.'

He shook his head maddeningly. 'Oh no, the terms of the loan were such that no pre-payment of the total amount is possible. I'm afraid you'll have to accept that you and I are bound together, if only financially, for some time to come.' He drained his juice glass and looked blandly across at her.

Serena stared impotently back. She had indeed examined her position very early that morning, and knew that without a further loan from the bank and perhaps a subsidiary loan from David, she had no immediate hopes of establishing Windfair's independence from Benedict's money. But wasn't it preferable to owe the bank and her fiancé than the man who had torn her life to shreds? That had been her reasoning, but now it seemed too impossibly hopeful.

'Isn't it possible to change the terms of the loan?' she suggested, forcing politeness although her fingers itched suddenly to come in contact with his smoothly shaved jaw. The only trouble with that, she sensed, was that she would be unable to stop flailing at him with her fists once started. Love turned to its opposite, hate, she'd heard; her hatred of Benedict simmered like an unlanced boil deep inside her, unmitigated by his plausible tale of a wife bent sickly on destruction.

'Unfortunately, for you, no,' Benedict answered equably. 'In fact, I've decided to make a home here on Bermuda for Debra and myself, and I shall be able to keep a close watch on my investment.'

Serena gaped unattractively. 'You're—going to live here?' she gasped.

'Why not?' he shrugged a nonchalant shoulder.

'I can write anywhere my travels take me, and this seems as good a place as any for Debra.'

'But the bank—surely you're not going to ...' Her voice trailed away, but her thoughts surged on. Surely he couldn't intend to throw up the position his ambition had led him to? Chairman of a prestigious City bank in London, his father-in-law's shoes still warm enough to bend to the shape of his feet!

Her thoughts must have been transparent. 'I married Caroline partly from ambition,' he said evenly, 'but the price was too high for me to hanker after the money and prestige I could gain through her. I stayed with her because—well, I suppose it was from pity, really. She'd never had a fair shake in life, given the family she was born into. A mother who drank herself into oblivion and a father who cared more for appearances than the emotional state of his wife or daughter. When Caroline no longer needed me, I told Sir Harold he could stuff the bank and I came out here.'

Serena drew a deep, quivering breath. He had lied to her once, what was to say he wasn't lying through his teeth now? Pat would have made a dramatic novel out of these ingredients ... mad wife, an equally mad girl-child intoxicated with life and love, a child filled with distrust of the adult world. But this wasn't a novel, some contrivance of an author's imagination, it was true experience, and Serena was too confused to think clearly.

The Carters came into the dining room, Frank loudly proclaiming his preference for a window table, unavailable for their dinner the night before. Sandra Carter nervously placated her son, who slumped, bored, into his chair overlooking the terrace. At another time, Serena would have been anxious to see that Windfair's guests, however obnoxious, were kept happy, but now she looked uninterestedly on the family trio who sat disgruntledly together.

'Your writing must have lucrative results,' she said dully, but with an element of question.

'It is. Roger Carson has reincarnated the classic detective novel,' Benedict intoned, obviously quoting from a review of his work. And of course she had heard of Roger Carson, even read some of his gripping novels of mystery blended with psychological motivation.

'You're—Roger Carson?' she asked numbly.

'The same. Luckily for me, people like to read about crimes committed for psychological reasons.' Benedict seemed amused. 'X murders his wife for the obvious reason that she's been indiscreet in her amorous propensities, but was it her husband who committed the crime or one of her numerous lovers—or a woman jealous of her ability to bind men to her in a sexual way?'

Serena's thoughts tumbled again, making her feel disorientated in a world she thought she knew. Benedict didn't need the fulfilment Caroline, through her father, had offered; he must be independently wealthy from the sales of his popular books. And that placed his loan for Windfair—where? In a niche reserved for moon-struck girls who had fancied themselves in love with him? Virgins he had unknowingly initiated into the exciting world of human passion?

'Benedict, I——' The words came thickly from her throat, too many other thoughts vying for supremacy in her mind. Did a man who incited the

passions of an unschooled girl possess the
sensitivity to care about a woman haunted by her
unstable background? The bleak greyness in his
eyes, the taut line of his mouth, suggested that the
possibility was there.

Relief flooded over her when David, trim in the
typical beige of Bermuda shorts and white open-
necked shirt, strode into the dining room. He was
so safe, so secure, so very normal that her smile
flashed with unconscious beauty as he approached
the table and came to drop a familiar kiss on her
cheek. Her eyes met Benedict's over David's
shoulder, and the grey bleakness in his caused her
smile to disappear. Shocked, she recalled that
Benedict knew nothing about David or her
engagement to him.

But she was wrong. David straightened and
nodded familiarly to Benedict as he pulled out a
chair for himself. 'Morning, Ramsey. Recovered
from our lengthy session last night?'

CHAPTER EIGHT

SERENA'S senses seemed to fragment into a thousand shattered pieces as she gazed, panicked, from one man's face to the other. It was impossible that they had met, purely by chance, without either knowing the other was involved in her life.

Then it came to her. Matty! And close on the heels of that thought came another. Benedict had deliberately sought David out last night—but why? David looked his usual unruffled self, and surely he wouldn't be sitting here calmly chatting to Benedict if he had any idea that the other man was the married one who had devastated her life years ago. There was a roaring in her ears that made it difficult to hear their lightly exchanged conversation.

'It's been quite some time since I indulged in that particular pastime,' Benedict admitted with a faint smile, indicating the empty juice glass beside his hand. 'That helped considerably.'

'Yes,' David agreed wryly, 'I resorted to the same kind of thing myself this morning.' He turned to Serena and grimaced. 'Perhaps I should have come over to see you last night as you wanted me to, darling. My head would have felt as if it belonged to me this morning if I had. It was such a hell of a day yesterday that I didn't put up much resistance when Ben here came along and suggested we talk over mutual friends.'

'M-mutual——?' Serena stared blankly at him, then down at the fruit dish John had just placed before her, going then to set down Benedict's eggs, toast and a large pot of coffee. The fruit was arranged in a magnificent, tempting tower shape studded with fresh grapefruit and orange sections, sliced Bermuda bananas, papaya, mango, but she knew her throat would close against swallowing any of it.

'Yes,' David resumed after ordering his own coffee from John, 'you remember the Gardners who were at Moongate a couple of months or so ago? I brought them over to dinner one night, they were so anxious to see Windfair.' He grinned. 'They must have liked it better here than at Moongate, since they raved to Ben about it when they got back to London. They've known each other for years, it seems.'

Ben! Serena herself had never even thought of shortening his name, it had seemed so distinctively his, but David's voice was almost affectionate as he tossed off the diminutive. There was something almost obscene in his open friendliness towards the other man, and she blamed Benedict for her fiancé's complete non-suspicion of the part he had once played in her life.

More importantly, it appeared Matty wasn't the guilty party in gossiping about the engagement. Benedict had known about it, probably, before coming to the islands. So why had he come, after remaining silent for so many years? Was he one of those men who made no effort until another man was interested? But there had been Caroline—until last week.

'Do you play tennis, Ben?' David was asking in

his friendly way when she once more jerked her attention back to the scene at hand. 'We can find another lady and make a foursome.'

Benedict looked up from the eggs he was devouring hungrily, his eyes blandly cool as they met Serena's. 'Afraid I'm badly unpractised,' he said with an odd inflection that seemed to mean more than the simple statement. 'Working in a bank leaves very little time for sports of any kind.'

'Never too late to start again,' David assured heartily, oblivious of the undercurrent flowing past him as he turned to Serena. 'How about it, darling? You could get Ben into action during the next few days and we'll arrange a match for early next week.'

Serena wanted to scream more than anything, her nerves frazzled to snapping point. Instead she sounded much as usual when she said, 'I'm sure Bene—*Ben* won't have any trouble in finding a bright young girl to practise with, one who's far less busy than I am.' Again the undercurrent flowed strongly, and she had the satisfaction of seeing a faint tinge of colour rise in Benedict's cheeks.

'Oh, come on, darling,' coaxed David, busy pouring coffee from the pot John had brought to him, 'surely you can spare an hour or two here and there from your painting. She's a marvellous painter, Ben, did I tell you? Everyone who sees her work wants to buy it as a reminder of their holiday in Bermuda.'

'I haven't seen her work,' Benedict's brows rose, perhaps remembering that he'd had no thought of examining her paintings when he'd been in the cottage the day before, 'but I'd like to. I knew a girl in London some time ago who showed a lot of promise in her art.'

Serena had no patience with this kind of verbal fencing, meaning concealed within meaning, and she rose abruptly, startling David when she said crisply, 'Shall we go into the office and discuss what I wanted to see you about?'

'But you haven't eaten your breakfast,' he said, justifiably bewildered.

'I'm not hungry after all. I'll ask John to save it for my lunch.'

'I really would like to see your paintings,' Benedict proffered, draining his cup and dabbing his napkin across his mouth before standing to look at her with what she felt was mocking politeness. 'I'll be looking for some for the house I hope to rent or buy here, and I'd like to see yours first.'

'You're thinking of settling here?' David, too, rose and looked delighted by the piece of news which Benedict had obviously withheld the night before. 'That's grand—and in that case, you must see Serena's paintings,' he smiled openly to her as he slid an arm around her waist. 'Our talk can wait for a few more minutes, darling, can't it?'

Aware that Benedict had somehow manoeuvred her into a corner she couldn't very well get out of without creating a stir, she nodded briefly and walked towards the dining room doors, David's arm falling uselessly to his side.

Benedict's ability with deception was firmly in place as they entered her studio cottage, not a muscle on his lean face betraying the fact that only yesterday he had dealt her one crushing blow after another there.

'Now look at this, Ben,' said David enthusiastically, lifting a rather large canvas on to a vacant easel. 'I suppose you're not yet familiar with Somerset Parish, but I can assure you there isn't a more faithful reproduction of this scene. The only thing I've seen to match it is a coloured photograph in a brochure the tourist office puts out. It's absolutely perfect as to detail.'

Serena wanted to scream again, this time to tell David not to be such a salesman, to recognise her work for what it was—commercial pap geared towards tourists to the islands. She was looking at it through Benedict's eyes, she realised, eyes that had looked with hers on the great masterpieces in the Tate Gallery, the National Gallery, and dozens of smaller galleries throughout London, his comments pithy and knowledgeable as they discussed the merits or otherwise of the works they appraised.

She wanted to die when he said of that first painting, 'Very pretty,' his voiced opinions reducing gradually to grunted acknowledgement as David displayed one picture after another. When the supply was exhausted, Benedict wandered over to the easel draped in obscuring muslin close to the window.

'What's this?' A twitch of his lean hand bared the shocking emotionalism of the work she had just completed, and David uttered a shocked exclamation.

'My God, Serena,' he breathed, 'surely you didn't paint this? It's—gross, meaningless. What on earth were you thinking of?'

She could have told him that the hot colours represented Benedict, the cool, steady ones, himself . . . but now wasn't the time for that. She would tell him when they were safely ensconced in her office that Benedict was the man she had loved once.

'I don't think it is meaningless,' Benedict remarked now, his head dropped to one side as he surveyed the harsh mingling of colour. 'To me it portrays passion versus cool sanity, equally balanced. Hard to tell where one leaves off and the other begins.'

'You see that in it?' queried David doubtfully, his own eyes following where Benedict's had led deeper into the painting. 'Well, it's certainly— different from anything you've done before,' he turned to look at Serena standing frozenly behind them as if re-assessing her meaning to him in a personal way. 'You've never struck me as a violently passionate person such as this——' he jerked a thumb towards the painting, 'implies you to be.'

'Don't we all maintain a façade over our emotions?' intervened Benedict smoothly, dismissing the painting as he turned to look at Serena intently. 'This picture is worth more than all the others put together. At least it possesses honesty, integrity, a striving after truth which the others lack.'

David, his eyes on Serena's face still, noted her barely perceptible flinch and rallied loyally to her defence. 'Now look here, Ben, Serena's paintings hang in living rooms and halls from Alberta to Zanzibar, and not one of those people would have bought that kind of monstrosity!'

'David, please,' she intervened, pained, loving his protective aggression but hating it at the same time. Because Benedict was right in his implication—she *had* prostituted her art by tailoring it to what the public wanted. She felt no guilt about that; the people who had bought her paintings would enjoy the nostalgia they aroused for years to come. If anyone had been cheated, it was herself. An artist should grow with every painting, seeing things that had been obscured before. She had stood still in one spot, repeating endlessly her first success. She agreed with Benedict, yet she hated him for his impersonal judgment of her work. He knew nothing of the struggles she had coped with in the early days of Windfair's revival, how vitally necessary the sale of her paintings had been to success. And yet, she reflected as they walked in taut silence back to the house, he must have known something about her efforts or he would not have advanced the loan so badly needed in the beginning.

'I'm sorry about that, darling,' David apologised when they went into the office after parting from Benedict in the hall. 'If I'd known he was going to be so bloody-minded about your work, I'd never have suggested showing it to him.' He put his arms round her and drew her stiffly erect body to him. 'Don't pay any attention to what he said,' he murmured huskily, 'he's probably one of those obnoxious people who know nothing about art but persist in spouting their opinions regardless.'

'You're probably right,' she agreed listlessly, wishing she could feel more than pleasantly comfortable in the circle of David's arms, realising too late that the moment had passed when she could have told him that Benedict's opinions on art and other subjects were long familiar to her.

'What was it you wanted to see me about so urgently, my love?'

'What?'

She looked up at him dazedly and he chided her softly, 'The reason you telephoned me late yesterday afternoon?'

'Oh.' She pulled away and walked to the far side of the desk, its bulk between them. 'I just wanted to know if you were aware of where the money came from to finance Windfair.' She kept her eyes steadily on his, watching for signs of guilt, embarrassment, but there was only puzzlement tinged with something else—impatience?

'The money? It came from the bank, of course. Serena, what's got into you? You haven't been yourself for some time now. Is it something I've done, or haven't done?'

'Of course not,' she denied quickly, forcing a smile. 'I'm sorry, I suppose I've gone on too long without a break.'

'Darling,' he came round the desk to pull her gently into his arms again, 'why don't you go off for a couple of weeks to the States? I agree, you do need a break, and you could start shopping for March or April.'

'March or April?' she repeated stupidly, her eyes scanning the warm brown of his for enlightenment, seeing instead a thoughtful gaze. Realisation dawned, and she gasped, 'Oh David, I'm sorry. We're being married then, of course.'

'Are we, Serena?' he asked quietly, the yellow motes that usually danced in his eyes strangely clouded.

'Well—of course we are. I'd simply forgotten that we'd rearranged the date, I'd grown so used

to the idea of June, I suppose I—still think——'
Her voice tapered off when she realised how over
apologetic she sounded. The telephone extension
shrilled an interruption, one she was ashamed to
admit was welcome at that moment.

'Mr Storey? Yes, he's here, just a moment.'
Silently she handed the receiver to David, envying
his ability to transport his mind instantly, alertly,
from one fraught scene to another.

'All right,' she heard him say as she wandered
over to the fireplace and stood staring down at the
fuchsia branches arching gracefully towards the
hearth, 'keep it going until the doctor gets there.
I'm on my way now.'

'Trouble?' she asked as he threw the receiver
back on its cradle and strode rapidly round the
desk. He halted in mid-stride and turned his head
towards her as if he had forgotten her existence.

'Yes,' he said grimly. 'One of the guests, a man
in his sixties, has had what seems to be a heart
attack on the tennis court. Why the hell they feel
they have to prove something here when they
haven't done more than walk to their cars for
years amazes me.'

'David?' she questioned faintly as he turned and
continued to the door, his brown eyes abstracted
when he looked at her from there. 'When will I see
you again?'

'I really don't know at the moment,' he said,
impatient to be gone. 'I'll telephone you tomorrow.
Meanwhile,' his eyes warmed, 'see what you can
do with Ben's game. I've an idea it would give me
a great deal of pleasure to chop him down to size,
if only on the tennis court!'

His ready smile was already fading when he

pulled open the door and went out, closing it firmly behind him. Serena stared at its blank face for a moment or two, then went to sit behind the desk, her fingers reaching for the ivory-handled letter-opener and twisting it back and forth in an abstracted motion. She should have told him about Benedict. That the opportunity hadn't arisen was hardly a feasible excuse; she should have made the opportunity long before now. The fact that she hadn't would make it seem as if she had something to hide from him, some residue of feeling for the man who had almost destroyed her.

Even David had sensed that Benedict should be brought down to size, a denting of the built-in confidence Benedict exuded like sweat from his pores. It was impossible to think that he truly intended to settle on Bermuda, her mind veered irritably. How could she be the wife David deserved while her one-time lover sat like a toad and watched from the sidelines? God, it didn't bear thinking about!

Pat looked up with a sunny smile when she paused by the desk. 'Good morning—or isn't it?'

'Not especially. Have you seen Mr Ramsey lately?'

'I think he went up to his suite after breakfast.' Pat gave her a worried look. 'Is anything wrong? I see Clive tried to find alternative accommodation for Mr Ramsey and his daughter.'

'Without success.'

Pat's sparkling brown eyes rested on Serena's closed expression. 'Is there any particular reason why you should want the Ramseys to leave?'

'Of course there is!' Serena snapped, gesturing with her hand round the time mellowed hall.

'There are other places far more suited to an eight-year-old child. She needs companions of her own age, and——'

'We've had eight-year-olds staying here before,' Pat pointed out gently. 'What's so different about this one?'

'Nothing, except that her father seems to think Matty has nothing better to do than act as child minder for him.'

'Glory be,' Pat murmured fervently. 'What bliss to have her attention diverted elsewhere!'

'If you need me I'll be in Mr Ramsey's suite,' said Serena, determinedly brisk, and turned away from the thoughtful, curious speculation in Pat's eyes. She couldn't have failed to notice the tension that filled Serena whenever Benedict was near during the past few days, and she was intelligent enough to know that the mere fact of Windfair being unsuitable for his daughter would never bring out the icy reserve in Serena's nature.

Damn Benedict, she fumed as she stepped quickly to the upper floor and strode purposefully to his door. He must see that the situation was impossible, that he couldn't stay here at Windfair or even on Bermuda. Her fingers rapped sharply on the panel, and without waiting for a reply she turned the handle and marched in, ready to do battle.

The small sitting room was deserted, and she hesitated before crossing to the bedrooms to her right. Perhaps he wasn't here after all, and the thought deflated the throbbing balloon of her anger. She had been worked up to the point where telling words and phrases would have come clearly and concisely to her tongue. Then she heard sounds from the bathroom tucked in between the sitting room wall and the tiny annexe bedroom where Debra slept. The door opened and Benedict appeared in its frame, naked but for the towel tucked loosely round his waist. His brows lifted in surprise, though the eyes under them took on a faint gleam of mockery.

'Well, you've timed your visit very well,' he said softly, coming into the bedroom and following her as she backed into the sitting room again.

'Don't be ridiculous,' she snapped, her vocal chords recovering from the shock of seeing him as she hadn't for six years, his lean body finely muscled and fit, the skin on his arms a darker hue than that on his shoulders and chest. For a moment she was taken aback by the involuntary rush of almost forgotten warmth that flooded to breasts and loins with breath-stopping suddenness. But now her eyes were glacial as they whipped over his. 'I'd have expected that you would shower before coming down to breakfast.'

'I did.' He straightened from the doorframe he leaned against and indicated one of the two overstuffed armchairs. 'Would you like to sit down while I slip into something less comfortable?'

'What I have to say won't take long.' She drew a deep breath, too conscious of the water drops that still clung, glistening, to his tightly packed shoulders and chest, droplets detaching suddenly to make zigzag rivulets on their way to the blotting towel that hung on his hips. Her eyes followed their course and seemed hypnotised, her mind grappling abstractedly for the words she had been sure would come so easily.

'You shouldn't be looking at one man like that

when you're engaged to another,' Benedict's voice insinuated itself softly into her mind, and her head snapped up.

'Don't flatter yourself,' she spat viciously. 'I was just wondering what I ever saw in you years ago. I must put that little aberration down to extreme naïveté, a lack of experience.'

His jaw tensed slightly, but his expression was unperturbed as he returned her look. 'It wouldn't happen now, I suppose,' he mocked, 'considering the vast experience you've accumulated since. Tell me,' he continued conversationally, moving to perch on the rounded arm of the settee set against the wall, 'did you sleep with anyone else before your fiancé?'

'David and I don't——' she began before realising that he had cleverly trapped her into the admission that sex wasn't high on the list of important feelings between them. Not as yet.

'That's what I thought,' Benedict said smoothly, 'and it's why I decided to stay on in Bermuda. You're no more in love with him than he is with you.'

'How dare you?' Serena breathed. It was all she could do, because her throat was closed with shock.

'Come off it, Serena,' he rose again impatiently, a flare of irritation glinting deep in the light grey eyes: 'People in love with each other deeply enough to think of marriage can't keep their hands, their eyes off each other. You two are like casual acquaintances—a kiss on the cheek, a disinterested arm round an equally disinterested waist. What kind of marriage do you think that's going to lead to? Or had you intended to have not only separate beds but separate abodes after the great day?'

His narrowed eyes missed nothing of the startled widening of hers. In fact, the question of where she and David would live after their marriage had never been settled between them; Windfair had the advantage of more space and privacy than the Moongate Inn could offer, yet David's life was centred there. It had seemed easier to shelve the problem and hope it would solve itself closer to the time of their marriage.

'Where we live is our business, not yours,' she hissed. 'In fact, not one part of my life is your business now, so why don't you go away and leave me alone? *That's* what I came to tell you,' she flung at him savagely, her heart thumping so hard she scarcely heard her voice, 'to get out of my life, out of Bermuda——'

'Oh no,' he shook his head maddeningly, effectively stemming her tirade. 'I went over to your fiancé's inn last night to gauge whether his attachment ran as shallowly as yours to him. I found that it did,' he ended grimly.

Serena licked her drying lips and stared at him in question. 'Why are you doing this, Benedict? *Why?*'

He returned her stare wordlessly for a long moment, then said slowly, 'Would you believe me if I said that I've been in love with you all this time, that I've never been able to forget you, that I've known from the beginning the struggles you've had to make Windfair a viable enough proposition so you could keep it?'

'No!' The cry was wrung from her frozen throat. To believe what he was saying was to negate the

years she had spent hating him, loathing the way
he had used her.

'That's what I thought,' he concurred levelly,
'and that's why I decided this morning that I'd
stay in Bermuda and conduct an old-fashioned
courtship.'

'You're mad!' she scathed, wishing she could
think of something more original, more damaging,
to say, but her thoughts were careening out of her
control, too chaotic to voice them in her normal
cool way. 'And insulting to David, not to mention
me. You think all you have to do is walk in here
and I'll fall at your feet, as I did once before. But
I'm not that silly little girl looking for grown-up
thrills now, Benedict. I'm in love with David,
whatever you think, and I intend to marry him.
He's kind, and generous, and he'd never dream of
posing as a single man to some naïve girl while
he's married to me.'

His flinch sent a surge of satisfaction through
her. 'I deserved that,' he said quietly, coming to
stand closer so that she could smell the soapy pine
of his skin, 'however mitigating my circumstances.
But don't you think I've paid my penance, Serena?
Six years of wanting you till I ached in every damn
pore of my body,' his tone changed to savage
bitterness, 'every day of those six years making the
hellish decision not to come to you, to throw
everything up and come to you. I almost went mad
when the Gardners came back and told me you
were engaged to marry somebody else.' Raw
emotion churned darkly in his eyes, like a cauldron
finally bubbling over, frightening her into silence.

'But I stayed . . . even then I stayed. I couldn't
leave Caroline alone with her madness. She needed

me as the focus of whatever devilish emotions drove her. If I'd left, she'd have disintegrated completely. I couldn't do that to her.'

His eyes dropped to the hands she had raised to his chest, and she herself was bewildered by the instinct of compassion that had brought them there. His skin was moist, not from the shower but from the sheen of sweat; her fingertips were sensitive to the abrasive dark hairs that curled under them, her nostrils to the pine-scented warmth emanating from his body. She must get away from here, from the stuffy smallness of the room that suddenly seemed to close in around her as Benedict loomed largely in her line of vision.

'Serena?'

She remained dumb as his hands slid behind the neatly tucked green striped blouse she had chosen to match her solid green straight skirt and drew her to the throbbing hardness in his thighs. 'Oh, mermaid,' he whispered huskily, 'you don't know how much I've wanted you!' His hips pressed out and down against hers, and Serena shivered as desire rose to envelop starved nerve ends that reached greedily to experience again the fulfilment they had once known.

Benedict's hands parted, one to run with intense fingertips down her spine, the other to raise the spastic rigidity of her head to the slow descent of his mouth. Tremors shook her when the hard, hot, seeking lips covered hers and forced the response she would have given anyway. Her arms circled the moist hardness of his body and coherent thought deserted her in favour of surrender to the exquisite sensations leaping from his mouth to hers, his body to hers. An exaggerated disappointment filled her when he pulled his mouth away and pushed her back from the waist at the same time.

'Oh, please,' she whispered, her throat thickened to admit a minimal amount of air, air that suddenly expelled itself when she felt the hurried fumble of his fingers at her blouse, the tug when it was detached from her skirt, the release of her bra and the soft swell of her breasts into the cups his hands formed for them. Her nipples swelled under the soft abrasion of his thumbs, hardening quickly as his mouth followed and shaped them into peaks of urgent desire.

She seemed to float on a sea of mindlessness when he bent and raised her easily into his arms, carrying her into the bedroom to the bed still tumbled from his sleep the night before. He completed her undressing before discarding the towel that hung even more loosely round his own hips, his eyes possessively greedy as they lit on the sensual swell of her breasts, the narrow indentation of her waist and the faint curve of her stomach.

'Oh, mermaid,' he whispered, 'you're the most beautiful creature God ever made.' He lay beside her, one arm arced above her head, the other blazing a trail for his lips to follow. Serena felt wanton, abandoned, as he deliberately roused the peak centres of her body to erotic awareness. She felt herself as a mass of quivering need, the soft skin of her breasts and thighs silken under his stroking fingers, thighs that parted sweetly to receive the tautened readiness of his body.

The telephone extension in the sitting room had been shrilling for untold minutes when Serena became aware of it. Then it cut like a particularly sharp knife that destroyed while it insisted on immediate attention. The glow in her sea-green eyes melted into the fevered grey of Benedict's eyes above her.

'It must be Pat,' she murmured faintly. 'I told her I'd be here.'

'To hell with her!' he cursed forcefully, sliding a leg across hers to trap her into immobility. 'I need you in a way David Storey never has,' he stated baldly, his mention of David's name being the catalyst that restored a semblance of sanity to her fevered mind. Whether Benedict's hold was not as firm as he believed, or whether she was given a strength beyond her normal capacity, seemed a moot point as Serena rolled from him and reached for the clothing he had so easily discarded. Her bra, panties, and slim-line skirt were firmly in place as she stepped into the sitting room and reached for the phone.

'There's a Mr Carter here,' Pat sounded relieved to hear her, 'and he insists on seeing you. Can I tell him you'll be down soon?'

'I'm on my way now.' Serena smoothed her skirt over the curve of her thigh. 'Thank you, Pat.'

'You're not going anywhere,' Benedict fore-stalled her as she went to the corridor door, leaping ahead of her and standing, a naked barrier, against it. The grey eyes blazed into hers ... a man thwarted at that stage of a sexual encounter would look like that, whether it was important to him or not.

'Move aside, Benedict,' she said almost wearily. 'I'm running a business here, and I'm needed.'

'*I* need you,' he countered savagely. 'Does that mean nothing to you at all?'

'At this moment, no.'

His jaw clenched, but he made no move to touch her as the expression in his eyes flared, then ebbed, much as the sensual cravings he had aroused in her were taking on a slower rhythm. It could have been an hour or a minute that they stood looking into each other's eyes, but finally he stepped to one side, allowing her access to the door.

Serena, once in the corridor, took time to repair the damage to her hair, her make-up, before going down to face an already curious Pat and the obnoxious Frank Carter. She was glad she had done so when the mirror revealed a woman recently made love to. Her lips bore traces of the strong, biting passion of Benedict's kisses, her hair had escaped its severe style in several places and hung in damp tendrils round her neck and temples. It took only moments to repair that minor damage . . . the haunted look in her eyes she could do nothing about.

'Oh, there you are,' Frank Carter exclaimed as she approached the desk, his tone implying that her time should be exclusively his. 'Your girl here doesn't seem to understand my very simple request that I want a car for the two weeks we'll be here. She keeps burbling on about taxis, but I'm damned if I'll pay one of her boy-friends to ferry us around when I'm able to do it myself at less cost!'

Serena had rarely seen Pat so incensed by a visitor to Windfair, and her own gorge rose in sympathy. 'My assistant, Miss Patricia Johnson,' she intoned icily, 'is perfectly correct in advising you that visitors to the islands may only hire licensed taxis, or mopeds which are the only means of independent transportation. We're a small island, Mr Carter, and chaos would follow if thousands of visitors were allowed to clog our already crowded roads.' She turned enquiringly to Pat. 'Are any of the taxi drivers on our list relatives of yours?'

'No.'

'Now look here,' Frank Carter blustered, 'I didn't actually say that——'

'What would you prefer, Mr Carter,' Pat enquired sweetly, lifting her pen, 'a taxi, or three separate mopeds?'

He seemed about to burst a blood vessel, but his voice was comparatively subdued when he bit out, 'A taxi, of course.'

Serena crossed to the door marked 'Private' as Pat continued her campaign to rub salt into Frank Carter's lacerated skin, closing it on '. . . just for this afternoon, or for a whole day?' as if Carter was compelled to watch every penny of expenditure.

A sudden revulsion against the myriad crowd that descended on Windfair almost year around caught her unawares. It hurt her that transient visitors had only a fleeting, surface, interest in the home of her forebears. It always had, but today the feeling was particularly acute. What would Charles, her father, have thought of his ancestral home being open to the likes of Frank Carter? He would have hated it ... but wouldn't he have hated more the thought of Windfair being sectioned under an auctioneer's hammer?

Oppression sat like an unwanted hat on her head, and Serena headed back to the hall. She would drive over to Moongate and see David. His easygoing charm was exactly what she needed at this moment.

CHAPTER NINE

THE Moongate Inn preserved the pre-cocktail, pre-dinner hush of any small hotel. Serena knew that David would be ensconced in his private apartments, readying himself for the enforced sociability ahead.

Nodding to the young man who was Clive's counterpart behind the desk, she walked on along the wide passageway leading to David's quarters. An attractive woman, her skin lightly coffee-coloured, passed her with a vibrant glance.

There was no answer to her tap on the door of David's suite, and she opened the unlocked door and stepped into the familiar sitting room with its comfortably upholstered chairs and couches. From the bedroom beyond with its attached bathroom came the sound of a shower being run full blast, and her mouth quirked wryly. For the second time that day she would be waiting to confront a man as he emerged from his ablutions . . . only this time there would be no devastatingly passionate scene to follow the meeting, as there had been with Benedict. She wandered over to the padded window seat that looked through diamond-shaped panes to the rose garden beyond, crossing her slender legs as she sat sideways to the window.

She would have to tell David just who Benedict was; it was the reason that had prompted her unexpected visit. Guilt sat uncomfortably within her, recognising as she did that her reactions to

161

Benedict's lovemaking sprang in part from the fact
that she had known no lover since him, when she
was young and inexperienced. There wasn't a
doubt in her mind that David could inspire that
same response once she let down the reserves that
had bound her for six years. He had been so
patient, and it couldn't have been easy for him. He
was an attractive man, good-looking, fit, muscular;
she had seen more than one woman cast longing
eyes in his direction, even when she was with him.

The hiss of the shower ceased, and when Serena
stood to walk back into the middle of the room to
let David know she was there, her handbag fell
from the window seat with a metallic clanking of
lipstick case against compact, the sound loud in
the sudden stillness.

'Clarissa?' David's voice came with unashamed
hope, 'Did you forget something?'

Serena bent to pick up her bag in a purely
automatic gesture. The face of the woman she had
passed in the corridor flashed into her mind, and
she knew fatalistically that the dark woman had
been with him here in the apartment, that they had
made love together. There was no time to identify
the sickening emotions that clawed at her for
attention; David, a towel straddled round his
waist, was staring at her in horrified disbelief, his
hair curving wetly over his forehead.

'For God's sake, Serena,' he found his voice
before she could summon hers, 'what the hell are
you doing here?'

She felt an hysterical urge to laugh, but
managed to suppress it. 'I—I came to tell you that
a—a somewhat similar scene took place in
Benedict Ramsey's suite an hour or so ago,' she

waved a hand towards the bedroom, 'and I felt so guilty about it I hurried over here to confess. Ironic, isn't it?'

'Now wait a minute, Serena,' he stepped further into the room, and she noted abstractedly that the water drops glistening on his skin left her totally unmoved, whereas with Benedict—but that could be the result of shock. 'Clarissa means nothing to me! She works for the tourist office and she came here to——'

'Don't, David,' she said, pained that he should dream up reasons for the other woman to be here when it was all too obvious she had come for one purpose only, and probably not for the first time. It was Serena's own sense of freedom, of a burden being lifted from her shoulders, that surprised her. She didn't love David, not in the way a woman accepts a man as her husband, she knew that now.

'What did you say?' he asked suspiciously, suddenly realising what she had said. 'You came here to—confess?'

'Yes. You see, Benedict Ramsey is the man I was in love with years ago,' she explained almost lightheartedly. 'He—had to stay with his wife for reasons I won't go into now, but as soon as he was free he—he came to find me.'

'And you're still in love with him?' David asked tersely, his eyes never leaving hers.

'I suppose I must be,' she said softly, half regretfully. 'I must say it makes it much easier telling you, knowing that you have—Clarissa? Now you can take her on the honeymoon you'd planned for us.'

'I've no intention of taking Clarissa on any kind of honeymoon,' he returned harshly. 'It's you I

want to marry, someone like you I've always
wanted to marry. The Clarissas of this world don't
expect marriage, a lifelong commitment. She was
useful to me as an outlet for feelings you'd never
let me express. That's all there was to it.'

'I believe you,' she said simply, her eyes a clear
green as they looked into his. 'You've always
wanted to prove something, to yourself or to your
father; marrying Serena Howard of Windfair
would have done that for you, wouldn't it? You
could be a man of standing then, not the son of a
drunkard who cared nothing for his business or his
life.'

She knew she had hurt him from the white
patches that appeared around his mouth and eyes,
but they also told her that she had spoken truth.
There was no victory to send her pulses beating
joyously, only a profound sadness that made her
want to weep. Could no man love her for herself,
not because she represented the brighter side of
life's coin from a mentally sick wife, or because
marrying her would bestow a longed-for status
upon the man concerned?

David spoke, but she didn't hear the words as
she snatched up her bag and went quickly to the
door. She was oblivious, too, to the smiles from
the Moongate staff members who recognised her
as she passed through the hotel and went to her
car.

The last person she wanted to see, next to
Benedict, was his daughter. But she and Matty had
arrived back from their lengthy shopping expedition moments before Serena herself stepped into
the hall.

'Oh, Miss Serena,' Matty greeted delightedly, though she looked tired and every year of her age, 'you've got to see what we bought today! Mr Ramsey spoils this child, but it's no more than your own daddy did to you.' She looked fondly at the child clinging to her skirts much as Serena had done herself many years before. 'Shall we show Miss Serena what we bought today?'

Debra peeped out from behind the housekeeper's voluminous black flowered skirt and shook her head. 'She's like my mother,' she pronounced negatively, 'she's not interested in what I wear.'

'Well, of course she is,' Matty contradicted, smiling even as she frowned in Serena's direction. 'Let's go into her office and she can look at them properly.'

With the aplomb of her years, she ushered the child past the desk where Pat sat and boldly opened the office door, sweeping Debra ahead of her as she looked back appealingly at Serena.

'I think she has you in a cleft stick,' Pat murmured, 'and for once I agree with her. That child needs a little loving attention.'

'Thank you, Dr Spock,' Serena said sarcastically as she followed the pair into her inner sanctum, turning back to add, 'I'm sure her father can afford a genuine psychiatrist, however.'

'That wasn't quite what I meant,' Pat retorted drily, rising and picking up the five or six paper bags Matty had deposited on the high-backed chair near the desk. 'Shall I order tea for you in the garden?' she asked innocently, carrying the packages into the room.

Matty, gratefully seated in the largest of the armchairs, answered for her. 'That would be very nice,' she acknowledged graciously, spoiling the effect by adding in a bossy rider, 'and some of those éclairs they were making this morning, for Miss Debra.'

Pat pursed her lips, then relaxed them again to give Debra a friendly smile. 'They'll be here by the time you finish showing Miss Howard your purchases.'

She had gone on her mission when Debra said in a low, intense voice, 'I don't want to show her my things, and I would rather have tea outside on the terrace.'

'You're going to have tea outside,' Matty returned firmly for once, 'in Miss Serena's special garden. There's very few people get to sit out there, just the very special ones she favours.'

Serena's temples had begun to throb hotly, and she was in no mood to cater to a mutinous child. 'If she'd really rather not——' she began, then saw a spasm of pain cross the old housekeeper's plump face. 'Matty, what is it?' she exclaimed, crossing quickly and kneeling down beside the chair, frightened by the ashy greyness under the black skin.

'Don't be—making a fuss,' Matty got out with only a trace of her usual asperity. 'That—dratted doctor gave me—pills, but I never took them before.'

Now wasn't the time to reproach the elderly woman for keeping a medical condition secret even from her. 'Where are the pills, Matty?'

'In—my room, top drawer of dresser.' Even Matty seemed afraid of what was happening to her now, and Serena knew she couldn't leave her. She had completely forgotten the small girl standing and looking on with widened eyes. Jumping to her feet, she half-ran to the door and wrenched it open, groaning when she saw that Pat was nowhere in sight.

'I know where her room is,' Debra volunteered in a strangely adult voice. 'I can go and find her pills.'

Before Serena had time to assent or deny, she had run to the door and disappeared. Serena fell on her knees again and looked anxiously at Matty, who seemed to be labouring for breath. Everything was happening in pairs today, she thought abstractedly; two men confronted as they came from the shower, and two heart attacks. She had no doubt that that was what Matty was suffering, just as the Moongate tennis player had earlier.

'Don't try to talk,' she urged when Matty struggled to form words. 'Debra will be here with your pills in a minute. You'll be all right, Matty, you've just overdone things today.' Damn Benedict, couldn't he have seen that Matty was too old to spend hours shopping with a child in the heat of the day? But how could she blame him when she hadn't known it herself? When it had never occurred to her that some day something like this would happen to Matty, that she wouldn't always be around as a cushiony link to her own past. She'd been selfish, she reproached herself silently as she looked anxiously at the still-ashen face and Matty's closed eyes. Oh hurry, hurry, Debra!

When the girl came back breathlessly moments later, Serena had already poured water from the carafe on her desk and held the glass to Matty's lips after taking one of the wafer-like tablets from the square box Debra handed her. The housekeeper swallowed obediently, then laid her head back on the cushions again.

'Thank you, Debra,' Serena whispered, 'you fetched them very quickly. Will you stay beside her while I telephone the doctor?'

Debra nodded silently and stood where Serena had kneeled, her small face solemn as she stared fixedly at Matty. Then she turned her head to look briefly up at Serena. 'Is she going to die?'

'Oh no, no.' Serena went to the telephone and dialled the doctor's number, her eyes resting thoughtfully on Debra's back as she stood guard on Matty. It was an odd question for such a young child to ask, and in such a collected way, but then her own mother had—'Doctor?' she said into the mouthpiece, thankful that he himself had answered the telephone. 'It's Serena Howard of Windfair . . .'

He was as soothingly calm as she was nervous. 'What has the old lady been getting up to now? You've given her a tablet, you say?'

'Yes . . . I think she's looking better already, but could you come and see her?'

'I can't get there for at least an hour,' he said after hesitating, 'but she should be all right until then. I suppose she's been overdoing things as I told her not to?'

'She—took a young guest of ours shopping for several hours today.'

'I'm surprised you allowed it, Serena,' he reproached with the familiarity of the doctor who had brought her into the world. 'As I told her six months ago, as long as she takes reasonable care of herself she'll outlive us all. I'm surprised,' he repeated, 'that you let her go on such an expedition.'

'I—didn't know,' Serena choked. 'She didn't even tell me she'd been to see you.'

'Stubborn old woman! Well, get her to bed and have her rest at least until I get there to put the fear of God into her. See you in an hour or so.'

Relieved, Serena returned the receiver to its cradle and looked at Matty again. If the doctor had suspected urgency, he would have come at the double. Indeed, the ashy colour had receded and Matty was sitting up and looking belligerently around her.

'I heard you talking to that doctor,' she accused, 'and don't believe a word of what he says. I was just tired, that's all . . .'

'Yes,' said Serena in the severest tone she could muster, 'and being tired means you have to rest. The doctor will be here in an hour, and it's me he'll blame if you're not nicely tucked up in bed. Come along, I'll go up with you.'

After a great deal of grumbling, the housekeeper was finally installed between the snowy white sheets on her bed, and glared at Serena as she went out to summon one of the maids to sit with her until the doctor came.

'I haven't had tea yet,' she complained fiercely.

'I'll send it up with whoever comes to sit with you. Coming, Debra?' She smiled at the child, who had insisted upon accompanying them to the bedroom, and after a hesitant glance at the mountainous figure in the bed, Debra followed obediently into the upper hall.

'It's my fault, isn't it?' she asked tearfully. 'If

Matty hadn't taken me shopping, she wouldn't have——'

'Oh, darling, no!' Serena exclaimed, dropping to her knees again, this time to pull the too-thin little body close to her in a reassuring hug. 'If Matty hadn't come with you, she would have been doing something else just as tiring. She's a very stubborn old lady, and thinks she can still do all the things she did when she was younger. Even if we'd tried to stop her going shopping with you she wouldn't have listened. Now let's go down and see about her tea before she gets up and stamps down to the kitchen herself.'

A slow smile of conspiracy reached Debra's eyes, and she tucked a confiding hand in Serena's as they went to descend the stairs. 'Can I take Matty's tea to her?'

'Yes, of course, but it's rather a heavy tray and one of the girls will have to carry it. Matty would be very pleased if you sat with her while she drinks it—and while she eats the éclairs she ordered for you.'

The grey eyes widened. '*She* was going to eat them?'

'Perhaps not all,' Serena conceded as they reached the hall, 'but she always had the lion's share when I was about your age. I kept it a secret, because she didn't want anyone else to know about her very sweet tooth.'

'I will too,' Debra promised solemnly, and Serena squeezed the fine-boned hand within her own.

Winning over a child was a heady experience, Serena acknowledged as she sat twenty minutes later under the spread of the poinciana tree in her private garden. In its way, more important than attracting a man and having him fall in love with the person he thought one to be. A child's eyes saw right through to the inner core of a person and weighed him or her in the balance of a ruthlessly honest scale.

For the first time, as she sipped on the second cup of tea Pat had brought to her, she had time to think of all that had transpired that day. But for the call to business matters, she and Benedict would have been fully realised lovers again, she admitted honestly. But that didn't mean she was in love with him in any more than a physical sense. To love completely meant absolute trust, and Benedict had destroyed that years ago. Just as David had destroyed her trust in him this afternoon. How many other Clarissas had there been in the years she had known him, in the months of their engagement? How many more would there have been had she married him?

'There's someone to see you,' Pat interrupted her reverie, her footsteps silent on the neatly clipped grass.

'Oh, it's probably the doctor?' The question hung fire on the moist warmth of the late afternoon air as Serena's eyes went beyond Pat to the stocky male figure marching through her office and down the steps to the garden.

'No, it's——'

'Miss Howard?' a brusque voice cut in. 'I'm Sir Harold Cranston, and I've come to collect my granddaughter.'

Serena had risen from the white wrought-iron chair and now froze into immobility. Pat seemed equally nonplussed as she looked from the iron-grey hair of the visitor to Serena's white cheeks.

'It's all right, Pat,' she said stiffly. 'This is Debra's grandfather.'

Pat withdrew reluctantly, sensing the fraught atmosphere the visitor brought with him but unable to disregard the obvious dismissal from Serena. She turned immediately when Serena called after her, 'Pat, would you see that we have some tea for Sir Harold?'

Serena indicated the intricately carved two-seater wrought-iron chair at right angles to her own. 'Won't you sit down?'

'I'm not here to exchange pleasantries, Miss Howard,' he said abruptly in a strained, but cultured tone. Still, he sat down where she indicated, looking vastly out of place in a formal clerical grey suit and grey pinstriped shirt. 'I've booked return flights to London on the night plane, so if you will see to the packing of my granddaugher's things we'll be on our way.'

He was a brusque, unpleasant man, the kind Serena reacted to with iciness. 'I presume you're talking about Debra,' she said evenly, resuming her own seat. She saw his marble-hard brown eyes sweep up the slender lines of her legs to her narrow hips and curving bosom, and shivered.

'My granddaughter, yes,' he nodded.

'I'm afraid I have no authority from her father to release her into your or anyone else's hands,' she said quietly. God, Debra sounded like a prisoner being bounced between two gaolers!

'Her father forfeited his rights over her years ago,' Sir Henry stated briskly. 'The child needs the stability I can offer—not that it's any of your business,' he added arrogantly.

'Perhaps not, but I wonder what kind of stability you provided your daughter,' Serena maintained her level tone. 'Forgive me if I'm wrong, but didn't she take her own life ten days or so ago?'

His thin lipped mouth narrowed into a pencil-thin line. 'You're presumptuous, but I'll tell you that my daughter took her life because she couldn't take her husband's infidelities any longer. I see he's exerted his usual mesmerism over you,' he sneered, 'in the same way he's made countless other women his victims. He spins them this story about his mad wife and how ill done by he is, and they fall for it like rows of ninepins. My daughter was as sane as you, Miss Howard, until she married him and had to put up with his constant womanising. It broke my heart just listening to her tell of his affairs, one even with his secretary, who was several years his senior. He's totally un-scrupulous, and you'd be wise to cut him out of your life right now.' He shook his head, a bear rebelling against caged imprisonment. 'My daughter would be alive today if she'd taken my advice long ago.'

Serena rose and paced restlessly across the grass, sickness churning in her stomach as she thought of Benedict's life as this man's son-in-law, his marriage to the beautiful but psychotic Caroline who had laid her fantasies at her father's door. If common sense had ruled instead of blind adoration of his marred daughter, Sir Harold would have known that Benedict had no need to resort to a woman several years his senior, as his secretary had been, if he had infidelity in mind.

She swung back, praying the right words would come to her.

'Sir Harold,' she began quietly, 'your daughter suffered an illness well-known in psychiatric circles. You let her marry Benedict knowing this, and I suppose it's understandable that as a loving father you closed your eyes to the inevitable outcome.'

'How dare you presume to judge my daughter's mental state?' he cut in abrasively. 'She was— beautiful, a lovely girl,' his voice switched to broken emotionalism, 'until she married *him*. Then she changed ... she told me about the late nights when he said he was working, the weekends when he made the same excuse. Times when I knew damn well he wasn't working, he wasn't to be found.'

'He wasn't with other women, Sir Harold,' Serena said woodenly, her gaze fixed on his bent head. 'He was writing books in a country cottage, books that were so successful that he could afford to ignore the carrots you dangled in front of his nose to persuade him to marry your daughter. You didn't know that the carrots weren't necessary, did you? He married Caroline because he loved her, and he stayed with her out of compassion, not because he wanted to fill your shoes at the bank.'

He raised his head. 'Books? What are you talking about?'

'Your son-in-law is Roger Carson, an extremely well-known detective fiction writer.'

'So that's why ...' He stopped and gave her a shocked look. 'My God, why didn't he tell me?'

'Would you have given him your support if

you'd known he had found a way to be completely independent of you and the bank?' she asked bluntly.

'No,' he admitted honestly after a pause. 'No, I wouldn't have. I'd have thought it was just another excuse for getting away from Caroline.' He seemed suddenly to remember her outside status. 'How is it you know so much about my daughter and her husband?'

How to answer that? Because I was once madly in love with your son-in-law while he was married to your daughter? No, a man like Sir Harold would find it impossible to believe that she hadn't known about Caroline.

'Because,' said Benedict from the opened glass doors leading to the garden, 'Serena and I fell in love a long time ago, when she was an art student in London. Yes, I was married to Caroline then,' he walked purposefully towards the other man, 'but Serena knew nothing about my marriage, or the hell it had become.'

Sir Harold was speechless for only a moment, then he rose to his feet, his ruddy cheeks coloured to puce as he faced his son-in-law. 'If it was hell, then it was a hell of your own making! With all your playing around with other women, you destroyed my daughter's faith in life! Why else would she have taken her own life?'

'Her faith in life was destroyed long before I met her,' Benedict said starkly, almost regretfully. 'You couldn't stand the thought of a child of yours being imperfect, so you ignored the illness that finally killed her.'

The arrival of the tea Serena had ordered for Sir Harold came as an anticlimax. And she had no

sooner gestured wordlessly to the wrought iron
table for the maid to lay down her burden when
Dr Harden breezed through the office and joined
the frozen group on the lawn. It was like a
situation comedy, one she wished devoutly not to
be involved with.

'Well, Serena,' he intoned in his booming voice,
'I trust you've sent that stubborn old woman to
bed.' Even his loosely arranged white hair
quivered with indignation. 'She's not getting any
younger, you know, and——'

'I'm aware of that, doctor,' she interrupted
hurriedly. 'May I introduce Mr Benedict Ramsey
and Sir Harold Cranston? Mr Ramsey and his
daughter are staying at Windfair for the time
being.'

Dr Harden nodded briefly to the two men,
seeming not to sense the antipathy between them
as they faced each other yards apart on the
emerald green of the lawn. His brilliantly piercing
blue eyes turned pointedly on Serena. 'There's
another patient far more ill than your Matilda that
I have to see at the hospital,' he informed her
brusquely, 'so if you'll take me to her, I'll examine
her.'

'Yes, of course.' Serena had no choice but to
follow the stocky figure back into the house,
leaving the young and old man still facing each
other in stiff positions. Relief mingled with
concern as she led the doctor across the hall and
up the staircase. Something told her that Sir
Harold Cranston wasn't a man to be thwarted in
his intentions. He had come to retrieve his
granddaughter from his hated son-in-law, and
nothing would budge him from his purpose. But it

was wrong, she told herself starkly. Debra needed the stability of a love her grandfather was unable to provide. Possession, blind indulgence, was all he could offer ... and look where that had led Caroline!

'Well,' said Dr Harden in his professionally hearty voice, 'I see you have an attentive nurse at your side.'

Debra sprang up from her bedside chair when they entered the room, her grey eyes reflecting the pride she felt at the doctor's comment. 'Matty's going to be fine,' she said defensively, although an element of fear made her voice more shrill than usual.

'I'm glad to hear it,' Dr Harden returned blandly. 'But perhaps you'll leave us alone while I confirm the diagnosis?'

Serena drew Debra from the room, smiling confidently down at her when they reached the hall. 'Matty's going to be all right,' she assured her gently. 'She's not going to die.'

'My mother did.' The bald words hung in the air between them for a long moment, then Serena touched her hand to the brown hair Matty had neatly arranged that morning.

'Your mother died because—well, she didn't want to be alive any more. It wasn't that she didn't love you, and your daddy, because she did, very much. She was ill, like Matty, but in a different way.'

They had reached the top of the staircase, and both pairs of eyes looked down on the scene being enacted in the hall below. Serena wanted to whisk Debra away from it, to shelter her in arms that had never felt maternal before. But it was too late.

Sir Harold's lacerating tone seemed to reverber-
ate around the high rafted ceiling. 'You killed my
daughter, and I'm damned if I'll let you ruin
Debra's life too! I'm taking her back with me
today, and not a court in the land will award her
custody to an immoral——'

'No!' Debra cried out, sliding from under
Serena's loose clasp at her shoulders and darting
down the stairs to draw up short by her father's
side. 'I don't want to go back to England with
you,' she defied her grandfather in a clear but
trembling voice. 'Daddy and I are going to stay in
Bermuda for ever and ever, and you can't make
me go with you!'

Sir Harold seemed too stunned to reply as he
stared palely at his granddaughter, and Serena
spared a pang of pity for the man who was now
completely alone in the world.

Benedict spoke then, too quietly for her to
discern the words, and she turned away and went
slowly away. She valued her own privacy too
highly to intrude on that family scene, though it
still blazed questions in her mind when she
dropped on to a window seat and stared out
without taking in the scene below. Why had
Benedict come out with that statement about their
love affair years ago? 'Serena and I fell in love a
long time ago,' he had said. But he hadn't been in
love with her, not in the way she had loved him.
She was the symbol of all he had missed in being
married to Caroline, a mere cipher in his life. Had
he wanted to give Sir Harold the impression that
Debra would now have a background of stable
parents who loved each other and her? No court in
the land, she wryly quoted Sir Harold, would

award a child's custody to her grandfather in such circumstances.

Benedict was using her again, as he had before and as David in his way had tried to use her. God, wasn't there one man in the world who valued her for herself alone? But what good would another man be when it was Benedict she loved, wanted? Her stance in his defence a few minutes ago in the garden hadn't been solely because she loathed the type Sir Harold represented, moneyed, titled, and arrogant to a degree. She still loved him, would probably always love him, but she had her own criterion now for the direction her life would take. Windfair was the biggest part of it, and she would be satisfied with the pride of possession and the security it promised. Men would come and go, but Windfair would last for ever.

CHAPTER TEN

SERENA wasn't disturbed in her cottage, although she half expected that Benedict would come to make trite explanations as to why he had made it seem to Sir Harold that their affair was continuing more strongly than ever. He had probably surmised that his father-in-law would pursue his granddaughter to Bermuda, hence the scene that morning in his suite. So it didn't surprise her when she went in to dinner, dressed in a high-necked gown of dark grey jersey wool, to find only Benedict seated at the Ramsey table.

She was mildly curious about Debra's whereabouts. Only a maid had been seated watchfully beside the frankly snoring Matty when she had looked into her room on her way to dinner. Had he mesmerised one of the other maids to sit by Debra until she fell asleep, as Matty had done until now?

'Oh, Miss Howard,' the male half of a couple from England called as she passed their table. 'We're enjoying our visit here so much,' he said as she paused and smiled, 'that we wonder if it's possible to extend it? I can manage another week if you can.'

'We'd love to have you stay on, Mr Prentiss,' she rejoined equably, 'but you'll have to see Miss Johnson at the desk in the morning, she knows every inch of space available at Windfair.'

'Fine, we'll talk to her, thank you.'

Serena continued to her own table, wishing she had taken her dinner in the office again after all. What appetite she still retained would be levelled by the consciousness of Benedict's presence in the dining room.

'Good evening, Miss Howard,' Joseph greeted her, smiling as he seated her. 'I can recommend the chef's special tonight—veal *scaloppini* served with baby potatoes and freshly minted peas.'

'Thank you, Joseph, I think I'll just have——'

'Miss Howard will have the veal, Joseph,' an authoritative male voice joined in, 'and would you please see that my meal is served at this table?'

'Yes, of course, Mr Ramsey,' said Joseph with automatic courtesy before looking in question at Serena. 'Miss Howard?'

Her eyes lifted to Benedict's leanly handsome features beyond Joseph's shoulder, and she nodded coolly. 'Very well, Joseph.'

Benedict was more suavely attractive than she had ever seen him. The white dinner jacket sat perfectly on his broad shoulders and contrasted well with his dark colouring. He also looked more carefree than any man had a right to be, considering his crushing dismissal of his father-in-law less than two hours ago. Resentment burned in her on the older man's behalf as Benedict familiarly took the seat opposite.

'I presume Sir Harold has left?' A sudden thought struck her, leaving her appalled. Had Debra gone with her grandfather after all? Whatever Benedict's faults, Debra was better off with him. 'Did he take Debra?' she blurted out with undisguised concern.

'No.' The gleam in his eyes seemed to intensify

slightly. 'She's upstairs, doing her damnedest to be grown up enough to put herself to bed.'

'Isn't she rather young for that?'

He shrugged and smiled. 'She evidently doesn't think so. My own opinion is that she's trying to impress you.'

'*Me!*'

'She's taken a three-hundred-degree turn where you're concerned,' he said, sounding eminently satisfied with that state of affairs. 'What happened today when Matty got ill?'

Serena frowned. 'Debra had to run up to her room and bring her pills down to my office—which she did very quickly and efficiently. In some ways, she's very mature for her age.'

'She got used to reacting quickly to her mother's needs,' he nodded more soberly. 'Caroline relied on her more than she should have.'

'Perhaps you did too.'

'Yes, I probably did,' he returned evenly, looking at her with an intentness that unnerved her. 'But taking Debra away from her would have destroyed her completely. She loved her to the fullest extent she was capable of——' he broke off to nod acknowledgment when Joseph laid melon slices covered with wafer-thin ham before each of them. 'My God, Serena,' he went on in a low, intense tone, 'you don't think I'd have left Debra with her if I'd thought there was the slightest danger, do you?'

Serena shook her head, unable to take her eyes from his. 'Your—wife was only concerned about your affairs with other women, right?'

'The affairs she thought I was conducting with other women,' he corrected grimly, reaching across the table to grasp the hand not engaged in lifting fork to appetiser plate. 'There were no affairs, Serena, outside her imagination. She even suspected me of casting lecherous eyes on my secretary, a middle-aged woman whose heart was broken when her husband died at the age of fifty-six. Caroline got it into her head that my fondness for Edith was something else, and she came to the bank and made a scene that was embarrassing for all of us. Her father believed all the fantasies she poured out to him, but I think now, for the first time, he sees the truth of how things were. He got on that plane tonight like a different man, and I can't put it down to anything new I said to him. It must have been something you said while you were talking out in the garden before I arrived.'

Serena frowned, wondering why anything she might say could affect Sir Harold to that extent. 'I didn't say anything really, except that—you've been independent of him and the bank for some time. Do you mind that I told him you're Roger Carson?'

He shook his head, his eyes greyly bemused as he looked at her. 'He'd have known eventually anyway. He said something else when he left to get on the plane.'

'Oh?'

Serena wasn't remotely interested in the appetiser she poked at halfheartedly with her fork . . . nor would she be able to stomach the veal to follow. Strangely, what she craved most was a double dose of a strong drink, although such a thing had never attracted her before.

'He said,' Benedict pursued, his fingers sensually provocative as they stroked the sensitive centre of her palm, '"You're damn lucky to have a woman like that in love with you. Bring her with you when you bring Debra to see me, which I hope you'll do whenever you can spare the time." Are you, mermaid,' he dropped his voice to a lower cadence, 'are you in love with me?'

Her throat closed on a sudden surge of pure emotion. 'Mermaid.' The word conjured up the steamy atmosphere of that arty café in Chelsea, her first view of him and the unusual colour of his eyes which had fascinated her immediately. Everything else seemed like a world apart ... her passing time until Joanna's love session had run its course. She remembered how she had tried to impress him with her own worldliness, implying that she too entertained men in the same way when occasion demanded. How stupid, how naïve she had been! Expecting Benedict to sense her inexperience, to make valid decisions based on what she had told or implied about herself. She had blamed him, nurturing a hatred that must surely have been directed partly at herself. If he had been less than honest about his marital situation, hadn't she been equally devious? A woman might starve emotionally before she found a man who had stayed, through compassion, with a wife it was impossible to love, like Caroline.

'I—think I am,' she said slowly, drawing her hand from his and looking at him squarely. 'But that doesn't make me ready to become the mother of an eight-year-old girl who had an unusual closeness with her mother.' She herself wouldn't have welcomed a substitute mother at eight or eighteen, she reminded herself bleakly. She had adored her father in the same way as Debra now adored hers, and she would have resented a grown woman ousting her from supremacy in his affections.

'Debra needs the opportunity to be the child she is,' Benedict said in a voice that twisted her heartstrings. 'Caroline reversed their roles, so that Debra was the watchful mother and she the capricious child.' He glanced at his watch as he straightened in his chair. 'I told her I'd check on her at nine and it's almost that now. While I'm gone,' he rose but still held her with his eyes, 'think about my love and that I want to marry you.'

He was gone before Serena had assimilated his words, and she looked up vaguely when Joseph appeared at her side and said reproachfully, 'You haven't eaten your melon, Miss Howard, and I was just about to bring your main course.'

'I don't want it, Joseph,' she said firmly, rising and setting off after Benedict, conscious but uncaring of the concerned frown the elderly black waiter sent in her wake. Nothing in the world mattered but Benedict and the answer she yearned to give him.

He had left the door to his bedroom open, and she looked beyond to where Debra, her body tiny in the full-length single bed, looked up at him with shining eyes.

'You didn't have to come, Daddy,' she said pertly. 'I'm all washed and in my nightie, and I remembered to brush my teeth.'

'Good. Now all I have to do is tuck you in and say good night,' he returned gently, bending to kiss the smooth forehead, his hands making a token gesture of tucking in the bedding around her slight form.

'Don't you know any bedtime stories?' she asked wistfully. 'I bet Miss Howard could think of one. Like the prince who searched the world until he found the princess because she planted roses round the cottage door.'

'I have another story that you might like,' Serena told her, stepping into the pool of light cast by the bedside lamp, and Debra gave her an animated look. Benedict had stepped back beyond the circle of light, but she was more interested in unwinding a tale that sprang to mind as swiftly as the one about the princess and the roses.

Sitting on the edge of the bed, she began, 'Once there was a beautiful girl, and the wicked . . .'

'You tell beautiful stories,' Debra sighed when it came to an end, her voice sleepily content. Almost before Serena had stepped away from the bed, she was asleep with the faint trace of a smile on her rose-pink lips.

'I'm glad the wicked stepmother turned out to be loving and kind in the end,' Benedict said huskily, his arms sliding round Serena's waist to draw her back to the taut line of his lean body.

Serena twisted within his grasp until she looked up, green eyes sparkling, into the shadowed grey of his. 'Did you think I'd give her a stepmother traditionally hostile?' she challenged, the answer she had sought to give him coming neatly packaged and complete.

'For God's sake, Serena,' Benedict bellowed across the deserted hall, 'tell that maid to leave my study alone! She's mixed up all my pages again!'

Serena came unhurriedly down the gracious curve of Windfair's staircase and walked tranquilly to her husband's irate figure at its centre. Her hands lifted to the smooth hollows of his shoulders, covered in a short-sleeved shirt of blue nylon that cast a bluish shade into his grey eyes. 'Don't fuss, darling. You know Matty puts the fear of death into her if she forgets to dust one level surface.'

'Then let Matty rearrange the level surfaces of my pages,' he snapped, then responded to the steady, unmoving gaze of her jewel like eyes on his. 'I'm sorry, mermaid,' the harsh lines around his mouth relaxed, his hand reaching for the gentle curve of her abdomen. 'Charles Howard Ramsey shouldn't be subjected to his father's fits of temper even before he makes his appearance, should he?'

She smiled enigmatically. 'Why not? He's been subjected often enough to his father's unbridled passion on occasion—speaking of which . . .' She took his hand and drew him towards the staircase.

'For a woman expecting a child in four months' time, you're extraordinarily lusty,' he complained, yet made no resistance as she led the way to the immense bedroom that had been theirs ever since Windfair had reverted to private status. 'Debra will be home from school at any minute,' he pursued huskily, his lips nonetheless unresisting as hers teased them into the hard wanting she was now familiar with.

'Debra,' she breathed against his mouth, 'has a rehearsal for the school play and she won't be home for at least an hour.'

Making love with Benedict was a new experience each time, and she suspected it would always be so. It was as if she had been dead for all those years until he came to her again, and now she felt

herself vibrantly alive, needed, wanted. Not only
by Benedict, but by Debra who, by a strange twist
of fate, now attended the girls' school she herself
had gone to just down the road from Windfair.
Debra, she thought tenderly as she cradled
Benedict's head between her burgeoning breasts.
How she had blossomed into a bright, loving
child, as eager as Benedict and Serena to surround
the coming baby with love and attention.

Fortune had smiled on her, she thought
abstractedly, her fingers playing with the clearly
demarked outline of Benedict's backbone. Pat
hadn't felt the dissolution of Windfair as a
guesthouse; she had married her dour teacher from
Oklahoma and wrote in her dry way that she
hadn't given up on converting him to the cause of
easy sociability. Joseph remained as gentle server
at their meals, although both chefs had moved on
to larger hotels. Jephra, their replacement, had a
wide repertoire of dishes both Bermudian and
European to replace them without difficulty.

'Darling?' Serena said in question when the
familiar heights had been scaled and Benedict lay
spent beside her.

'Mmm?'

'Don't you think Peregrine Howard Ramsey
sounds rather good?'

Benedict raised himself on an elbow to look
with grey mockery into her sea-green eyes. 'Perry
would be all right, but what if it's Perrina?'

Perrina, she thought, savouring it. Yes, it had a
different ring about it . . .

Here's how to get this special offer from Harlequin! As simple as 1…2…3!

1. Each month, save one Treasury Edition coupon from your favorite Romance or Presents novel.
2. In four months you'll have saved four Treasury Edition coupons (<u>only one coupon</u> per month allowed).
3. Then all you have to do is fill out and return the order form provided, along with the four Treasury Edition coupons required and $1.00 for postage and handling.

EYE OF THE STORM

MAURA SEGER

A powerful
portrayal of
the events of
World War II in the
Pacific, *Eye of the Storm* is a riveting story of how love
triumphs over hatred. In this, the first of a three-book
chronicle, Army nurse Maggie Lawrence meets Marine
Sgt. Anthony Gargano. Despite military regulations
against fraternization, they resolve to face together
whatever lies ahead.... Author Maura Seger, also known
to her fans as Laurel Winslow, Sara Jennings, Anne
MacNeil and Jenny Bates, was named 1984's
Most Versatile Romance Author by *The Romantic Times*.

*You're invited to accept
4 books and a
surprise gift Free!*

Acceptance Card

Mail to: **Harlequin Reader Service®**

In the U.S.
2504 West Southern Ave.
Tempe, AZ 85282

In Canada
P.O. Box 2800, Postal Station A
5170 Yonge Street
Willowdale, Ontario M2N 6J3

YES! Please send me 4 free Harlequin Romance® novels and my free surprise gift. Then send me 6 brand new novels every month as they come off the presses. Bill me at the low price of $1.65 each ($1.75 in Canada)—an 11% saving off the retail price. There are no shipping, handling or other hidden costs. There is no minimum number of books I must purchase. I can always return a shipment and cancel at any time. Even if I never buy another book from Harlequin, the 4 free novels and the surprise gift are mine to keep forever.

116 BPR-BPGE

	(PLEASE PRINT)	
Name		

Address		Apt. No.

City	State/Prov.	Zip/Postal Code

This offer is limited to one order per household and not valid to present subscribers. Price is subject to change.

ACR-SUB-1

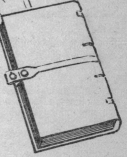